For more than forty years,
Yearling has been the leading name
in classic and award-winning literature
for young readers.

Yearling books feature children's
favorite authors and characters,
providing dynamic stories of adventure,
humor, history, mystery, and fantasy.

Trust Yearling paperbacks to entertain,
inspire, and promote the love of reading
in all children.

THIRTY CHILLING TALES
SHORT & SHIVERY

Retold by ROBERT D. SAN SOUCI

Illustrated by KATHERINE COVILLE

A YEARLING BOOK

Published by Yearling, an imprint of Random House Children's Books
a division of Random House, Inc., New York

Visit us on the Web! www.randomhouse.com/kids

Educators and librarians, for a variety of teaching tools, visit us at
www.randomhouse.com/teachers

ISBN: 0-440-41804-6

Reprinted by arrangement with Doubleday Books for Young Readers

Printed in the United States of America

September 2001

10 9 8 7

ACKNOWLEDGMENTS

Grateful acknowledgment is made to the following for permission to adapt their copyrighted material.

"The Witch Cat" is based in part upon the tale of the same name in *Ghosts of the Carolinas* by Nancy Roberts, copyright 1962, 1967, and used with the kind permission of Bright Mountain Books, Asheville, North Carolina.

"The Ghostly Little Girl" is based on a story by Randall A. Reinstedt that appeared in Mr. Reinstedt's *Ghostly Tales & Mysterious Happenings of Old Monterey,* copyright 1977, used with the permission of Ghost Town Publications, Carmel, California.

"The Skeleton's Dance" is based, with the permission of the University of Chicago Press, on the story "The Skeleton's Song" in *Folktales of Japan,* edited by Keigo Seki, translated by Robert J. Adams, copyright 1963.

"Scared to Death" is based, with the permission of the University of South Carolina Press, on the story "The Leaning Tombstone" in *Charleston Ghosts* by Margaret Rhett Martin, copyright 1963.

To Al Schroeder,
who loves a scary story
almost as much as the author.

R.S.S.

Contents

Introduction

Welcome! Since you've taken a look in this book, I guess it's safe to assume you like to read spooky stories. I must admit that I enjoy a good shudder myself. The thirty stories in this book will introduce you to ghosts, goblins, and assorted other monsters. But beware! These creatures that are lurking in the shadows along a deserted street, or glimpsed in a lightning flash outside your window on a stormy night, or have just put a claw on the knob of the door into this room *(gotcha!)* are pretty creepy customers. Before you read any further, you might want to turn up the lights a bit or hang a clove of garlic on the wall.

Just in case. . . .

Over the years, I've read or heard hundreds of spooky stories, and I have found that some of the best are folktales that have been shared by people in moonlight or candlelight or electric light—sometimes for hundreds of years or more. Many such tales were handed down from storyteller to storyteller countless times, before someone finally wrote them down. Often they were changed slightly with each retelling, as a storyteller added his or her own details and a bit of local color. But the heart of such a story remains the same no matter how many different ways it's told: it has the power to capture our imaginations, give us a thrill of excitement (and chill us at the same time), and make us look at ourselves and our place in the world in a different way. And it might just reassure us that good can triumph, evil doesn't go unpunished, and courage can help us face down even the most frightening monsters.

The stories here come from many different times, from a variety of cultures, and from countries all around the world; but they have one thing in common: they're scary. In these pages, you'll encounter a dancing Japanese skeleton that tricks a murderer . . . a Russian vampire who plagues a peaceful village . . . a Canadian werewolf who haunts a winter forest by moonlight . . . a haunted gold mine in the Old West . . . a clay statue that comes to life . . . a ghost in Iceland, who returns from the dead to claim his bride . . . a goblin pony that takes its riders on a fearful Halloween journey . . . a boy who spies on a witch in colonial America and learns the terrible price of meddling with black magic . . . a brother and sister who battle an African demon . . . and a monster so strange that everyone sees it differently and no two people can agree what to call it.

I've retold these stories in my own way. Sometimes I've just changed or added a few details, shortened a very long tale, or made the old-fashioned language a bit easier to understand, as in the case of Washington Irving's fearsome "Adventure of the German Student." Sometimes I've taken a very brief incident and expanded it to a full-length story, to satisfy my own curiosity about what *might* have happened to the people in the story if the original storyteller had told it in a slightly different way. The story of "The Ghostly Little Girl" and her three best friends is a good example of taking an account that was only a few paragraphs long and making it into a longer story.

Sometimes I have combined several very short tales into a single story: "The Hunter in the Haunted Forest" weaves together into a single narrative three brief Teton Sioux stories of warriors who met ghosts when they were alone in the wild. Once in a while, as with the legend of the *Cegua*, a Central American demon which haunts the roads by night and drives travelers mad with its horrible appearance, I have used a description of the creature and its history as the basis for spinning my own, original story around such lore and legend.

What I've tried to do is make these stories my own, and share them in a way that you, the reader, can enjoy them and make them *your* own. I hope you'll have as much fun discovering these shivery tales now, as I did finding them earlier, and retelling them. For those of you who want to know more about the background of individual stories, I have included "Notes on Sources" at the end of this volume.

So, happy reading! And if you think you hear something scratching at the window or a footstep in the empty room overhead, just remember, it's only your imagination.

Probably.

The Robber Bridegroom

(adapted from the Brothers Grimm)

There was once a miller who had a beautiful daughter. He was a hard worker, so his business prospered, and he grew wealthy. A widower, he gave his only daughter fine dresses and shoes with silver buckles. For himself he bought a splendid cloak, a broad-brimmed hat with a huge ostrich feather, and a gold ring with a picture of his mill engraved on it, because this had brought him his riches.

One night, however, robbers broke into the mill, and stole his hat, cloak, and ring—and all the gold he had saved up. Then the old man said to his daughter, "You must marry soon. The world is full of wicked men, and you should have a husband to protect you. But he must be a wealthy man, because you deserve the fine things I can no longer buy you."

"I don't care if the man is rich or poor," said the girl, Elsa, "as long as I love him and he loves me."

"Tut," said her father impatiently, "if the right kind of bridegroom comes along and asks for your hand, I'll let him marry you."

Soon enough, a suitor turned up who was dressed in the

finest clothes, had boots with silver toes and tops, and rode a grand horse with a bridle trimmed in gold.

"I have seen your daughter when she walks to the village," said the stranger, "and I want her to be my wife."

The miller was dazzled by the man's garments and his horse's trappings, so he said, "She will be your wife."

But Elsa didn't love him as a bride-to-be ought to love her future bridegroom. She didn't trust him; and whenever she looked at him or thought about him, a shudder ran through her.

The stranger came often to the miller's house. Finally, he said to Elsa, "You're engaged to me, and yet you have never been to see me."

"I don't even know where your house is," the young woman answered, feeling a sudden chill in her heart.

Her suitor said, "My house is in the depths of the forest."

"Then I could never find my way there," Elsa said.

"Nonsense," said the stranger. "Next Sunday, you must come and see me. I've already invited some other guests, who are eager to meet you. So that you can find the way, I'll leave a trail of ashes to guide you."

Elsa started to protest, but her father said, "Tut!" Then to the richly dressed stranger he said, "She will be there. I will see to it."

When Saturday came, the girl was about to start out, because her bridegroom had told her the journey would take a day and a night on foot. She felt terribly frightened, though she did not know why. To be sure of finding her way back, she filled her pockets with dried peas and beans to mark her path. At the entrance to the forest, she found the trail of ashes, like a thin, gray thread, and followed it deep into the dark woods. But every step or two, she tossed a few peas and beans to her right or left.

She walked nearly that whole day and night, all the way into the heart of the forest. In the morning, which was almost as gloomy as midnight, she saw a house set by itself in a small clearing. It was so dark and dismal that she feared going any closer. But the trail of ashes led right to the front door, so she went up.

Elsa knocked softly several times; when no one answered, she went in. She saw nobody; there was a silence over all the rooms.

Suddenly, a voice cried:

> "Turn back, young woman! Run away!
> You've come to a robber's house this day."

She looked up and saw that the voice had come from a bird in a cage that was hanging in a window. Once more, it warned her:

> "Turn back, young woman! Run away!
> You've come to a robber's house this day."

She was about to turn and run, when she heard someone singing in a sweet, clear voice deep in the house. The voice was so gentle and sad that Elsa had to see who was singing. She followed the sound from room to room, all over the house, but they were all empty. At last she reached the cellar door. Descending the steep and narrow steps, she found an old blind woman who was sitting in a corner, shaking her head sadly, while she sang mournfully to herself.

"Who are you?" Elsa asked.

"I keep this unhappy house," explained the blind woman. "But what are you with such a young, kind voice doing here?"

"I'm to marry the master of the house," said Elsa.

"Alas! You poor child! You have no idea where you are. You're in the den of a thief and a murderer. Years ago I was brought here with a promise of marriage. Instead the villain blinded me so I could not run away, and has made me work harder than the most wretched slave. Now that I've grown weary and unable to work as I once did, he has brought you here. He will drive me into the woods to die, and he will blind you and make you take my place."

"Come with me," urged Elsa, "we'll run away together."

But as she was guiding the older woman toward the steps, they heard the sound of rough voices above. When Elsa recognized her bridegroom's voice, her heart sank.

But the old woman said, "Hide behind those chests in the corner, and be quiet as a mouse. Don't move, or everything is lost. Tonight, when the robbers are asleep, I'll fetch you. Then we can escape together."

Hardly had Elsa hidden behind a metal-bound chest, when the chief robber came to the head of the stairs and bellowed, "Come up and fix us dinner, or you'll regret it quick enough! My bride hasn't come, and I'm in a rare bad temper. In the morning, I will ride to demand my bride and have no more of these games! Her father is a greedy and foolish man; he will hand her over. And it's going to be harder for her than she can imagine, since she has disobeyed me. Now, hurry and set out some food and drink."

All through the afternoon and evening, Elsa listened to the roaring and stamping and laughter as the men grew drunk and began to argue among themselves. Hidden behind the chests, she trembled and shivered, dreading her fate if she were discovered.

Now one chest that was near her hand was partially opened; she could see gold gleaming faintly in what little light fell down through the open cellar door. Carefully Elsa

lifted out several coins, a belt buckle, and a brooch, all of finest gold. Then, reaching in more deeply, she discovered a massive gold ring with the picture of her father's mill engraved on it. She knew in a moment that these robbers were the ones who had stolen all their gold months before.

Keeping quiet, she dropped the ring in her skirt pocket. Then she waited, while the sounds above continued, though it was growing later and later. She began to fear the robbers would go on crashing about until morning, and the old woman's plan would fail.

Upstairs, however, the blind woman put a sleeping potion in the thieves' wine. Soon, one by one, they lay down and went to sleep, snoring loudly.

When they were all asleep, the housekeeper called down to Elsa, "Come quickly! We must hurry!"

The girl hastily came out from behind the chests and climbed the stairs. She had to step over the sleepers, who lay in rows upon the floor. She was dreadfully afraid of touching them, for fear one would wake, but she got through without mishap.

The other woman was waiting by the open door. Elsa took her hand, and they hurried away as quickly as they could from the robbers' den.

All the ashes had been blown away by the wind, but the peas and beans, being heavier, remained to show them their way in the moonlight.

They walked the whole night and reached the mill the next afternoon. There Elsa told her father everything she had been through and the plan she had for trapping the wicked thief. Then her father hastened to the village to invite all his friends and relations to a feast, while Elsa and the blind woman set out tables and cooked every bit of food in the house.

When the robber and his men rode up to claim Elsa, the

miller welcomed them with a great show of friendship. "My daughter will go away with you this very day," he said, "but first, share a meal with us in honor of my daughter's wedding."

The robbers, who had awakened to find their housekeeper gone, and had been forced to scrounge a wretched breakfast for themselves, were only too glad to sit down and enjoy themselves.

During the meal, the miller asked each person to tell a story to entertain the other guests. When it came Elsa's turn, she was silent. But her bridegroom said, "Come, my sweet, you must tell us a story, too. I won't have people thinking my bride is a dull wit."

"Very well," the girl said, "I will tell you a dream I have had. In it I was walking alone in a gloomy wood, and I came to a solitary house, where not a soul was to be seen. A cage was hanging in the window of one of the rooms. In it was a bird which cried:

> "Turn back, young woman! Run away!
> You've come to a robber's house this day."

"It repeated the same words twice."

"I don't think I care for this story much," grumbled the bridegroom.

"This was only a dream, my love!" protested Elsa. Then she continued, "I heard someone singing a sweet song, so I walked all through the rooms, but they were empty. At last I went down to the cellar, where I found a blind woman singing to herself. When I told her I had come to marry the master of the house, she cried, 'Alas, you poor child! You're in the den of a thief and murderer!' Then she told me how he planned to blind me, and make me a slave in her place."

"Be quiet! I've had enough of this foolishness!" shouted the bridegroom, rising in his seat.

"This was only a dream, my love!" said Elsa. Then she quickly went on, "The robbers returned at that moment, so the old woman hid me behind some chests in the cellar. While they were making merry upstairs, I looked in one of the chests and discovered—"

"Silence!" bellowed the bridegroom, drawing his dagger to threaten the girl. But she bravely finished, "I discovered a gold ring, with a picture of this mill on it! The ring that belonged to my father and was stolen by robbers months ago! *And here is that ring!*"

So saying, Elsa produced the ring and showed it to the company.

When the bridegroom heard these words, he turned pale as ashes and tried to escape, his men with him. But the guests seized them all and turned them over to the king's soldiers, who took them away and had them hanged for their crimes.

Jack Frost

(from a Russian folktale)

Once upon a time there was a widow who had a daughter of her own and a stepdaughter. Whenever her own daughter said or did anything, the woman would pat her on the head and say, "Clever girl!" But no matter how hard the stepdaughter tried, she was always being called "foolish" or "lazy" by the woman, who often scolded her and sometimes beat her.

The truth of the matter was that the stepdaughter, Maria, was kind and beautiful, while the woman's own daughter, Yagishna, was plain and selfish. But her mother saw only what she wanted to see, so she praised Yagishna continually and made Maria's life a misery. Even an angry storm blows itself out at last, but the old woman's hatred for her stepdaughter never lessened. She said one cruel thing after another, and she was forever grabbing Maria by the collar of her dress to shake her for being "such a burden on us."

One day, in the dead of winter, the stepmother made up her mind to have done with her stepdaughter. She told her aged servant, "Old man, take Maria into the open field where the bitter frost is the thickest and leave her there. I don't want to set eyes upon her or hear her voice ever again. And if you value your life, don't take her to the warm house of your relatives."

The old man begged her not to force him to do such a wicked thing, but the stepmother would not relent. Because he knew that his family would starve if he lost his job, he put the girl on a sled. He tried to cover Maria with an old horse cloth, but Yagishna saw this and snatched it away with a sharp laugh.

"Do as my mother says, or you'll find yourself and all your children out in the cold along with her," she said nastily.

Heavyhearted, the old man drove Maria out to the open fields near the edge of the forest. He set her down on a heap of snow, hugged her, then hastened home as fast as possible, so that he wouldn't see the child's death.

Poor little Maria remained where she was, shivering and softly saying some prayers. Suddenly a strange-looking man came leaping and jumping from the forest toward the girl. He wore a greatcoat of silver-white fur, a high peaked cap of the same silvery fur, and boots of white leather worked with silver. He had thick white eyebrows and a bushy white beard, while his nose was as red as an apple. His coat and hat were spangled with diamonds, and silver bells on a white ribbon across his chest jingled as he bounded toward Maria.

"Little girl, little girl, I'm Jack Frost, the Ruby-Nosed," he said. "I bring the winter wherever I go."

"Oh," she said sadly. "Welcome, Jack Frost! God must have sent you to take me away from this world. It will be hard to leave, for it all looks so beautiful today: the snow is so white and the air is so clean and the ice sparkles like diamonds."

Now he was about to touch her body and freeze her to

death, but he was moved by her wise words and sad eyes. Instead he reached into one of the immense pockets of his greatcoat, pulled out a fur coat, and tossed it to Maria.

She quickly put it on, then squatted on her heels. Sitting in the snow, she watched while Jack Frost went leaping and jumping back to the edge of the forest. In a twinkling, he was back, carrying something in his arms. "Little girl, little girl, I'm Jack Frost, the Ruby-Nosed," he cried. "I have brought something for you."

"Is it my death?" Maria asked fearfully.

But he had not returned to take her life away. He brought her a chest, heavy and deep, and filled with bedding and petticoats and all sorts of warm clothes.

Then Maria sat on the chest in her fur coat, laughing and clapping while Jack Frost danced for her.

A third time he bounded away to the forest's edge; this time, when he came back, he gave her a cloak embroidered with silver threads and studded with pearls and diamonds.

Wonderingly, Maria drew this cloak over her fur coat. She looked as beautiful and elegant as a grand duchess. For a long time she sat there happily singing songs, while Jack Frost danced lightly over the sparkling ice and snow.

Meanwhile, her stepmother said to her servant, "Go, old man, and bring home my daughter so that we may bury her." Then she set about fixing the evening meal for herself and Yagishna.

A short time later, the gate creaked, the doors flew open, and the old servant dragged in a chest, heavy and deep. Maria followed, radiant and regal as a princess.

When the stepmother saw all the riches Maria had returned with, she immediately set an extra place at the table for the girl. She sat her stepdaughter down, pretended to ask her forgiveness, made a great show of giving her the daintiest morsels (even though Yagishna complained about this), until she had gotten the whole story out of Maria.

As soon as Maria was asleep, the old woman called her servant. "Old man," she ordered, "harness the horses and have them ready to go at the first light of dawn. Take my daughter to the same field, in the very same place, and leave her there. Then return for her in the evening, to gather up the treasures she will receive."

In the morning, the old woman struggled to awaken her daughter.

"Let me sleep," complained Yagishna. "It's too cold to do anything else."

"You must go and get treasures from Jack Frost, you lazy creature," her mother scolded.

"Can't we just take Maria's gifts for ourselves?" asked her daughter crossly.

"We will, we will," said her mother impatiently, "but why settle for one treasure when we could have two? Now, get up!"

Grumbling, Yagishna did as she was told. She put on her warmest coat and hat and boots. When she was on the sled, her mother bundled her up in furs and blankets. Then the old servant drove her to the field and left her there, just as the morning sun turned the ice crystals bright as diamonds.

Yagishna sat on her pile of furs and tried to keep her eyes open.

Suddenly Jack Frost came prancing from the edge of the forest.

"Young woman, young woman, I am Jack Frost the Ruby-Nosed," he said.

"Then be quick and bring me a treasure," said Yagishna, who thought he looked foolish with his leaping about and

jingling bells and nose like an apple stuck to the front of his face.

"Young woman, young woman, I am Jack Frost the Ruby-Nosed," he repeated. "I bring the winter wherever I go."

"When you've brought me my treasure," said Yagishna disagreeably, "you can go, and take winter with you. It's ugly and cold. Now, where is my gift?"

"Young woman, young woman, I am Jack Frost the Ruby-Nosed," he cried, dancing closer to the girl. "And here is your gift of diamonds and silver."

And he stretched out his hands to Yagishna.

In the evening, while Maria stoked the fire, her step-mother anxiously watched the door for the return of her daughter.

Suddenly she heard the creak of the gate outside. Without waiting, she flew to the door and saw the old servant standing beside the sled, cap in hand. Impatiently the old woman pulled at the mound of furs on the back of the sled.

"Yagishna, foolish child, come out from underneath. You'll be warm inside in a minute, but first show me your treasure."

To her horror, when the woman pulled back the last fur, she saw her daughter lying there, a cold corpse. Silver snowflakes frosted her eyelashes, and ice like diamond chips beaded her lips where her last breath had frozen.

The shock was too much, and the greedy stepmother fell down dead in the snow.

Maria became mistress of the farm, where the old servant continued to serve her faithfully all the rest of his days.

The Waterfall of Ghosts

(from the Japanese writings of Lafcadio Hearn)

There was once a small village in Japan very near a cascade called the Waterfall of Ghosts. No one could say for sure why it was called this. Some people thought they saw the twisting shapes of ghosts in the mists that rose from the rocks onto which the water poured; some claimed to hear ghostly voices—or the voices of gods or demons—in the roar. It was considered a holy place, so the villagers built a small shrine at the foot of the falls and left a little wooden money box there for visitors to make offerings.

One frosty evening in the last century, the women and girls who worked in the local factory, where they spun hemp into lengths of rope, gathered around the big iron stove after their work was done.

As they warmed their hands by the coal fires, they amused themselves by telling ghost stories. By the time a dozen stories had been told, even the bravest began listening with new ears to the whisper of wind at the doors and window frames. They began to grow uneasy at the idea of walking home through the dark.

Then one of the younger girls, who was enjoying the

little thrills of fear she was getting, said, "Just think of going all alone tonight to the Waterfall of Ghosts!"

Her suggestion provoked shudders, followed by nervous laughter.

"Why," said the girl, unwilling to let the matter rest, "I'll give all the hemp I spun today to any person who goes!"

"So will I!" exclaimed another, caught up in the spirit of the game.

"And I!" another promised.

Soon all but one of the women had offered her day's output of rope as a prize to anyone brave enough to go to the waterfall that night.

The only spinner who did not join with the others was a young woman named O-Katsu, the wife of the village carpenter. "Listen," she said, "if you will all really agree to hand over the hemp you spun today, I will go to the Waterfall of Ghosts."

Her words were met with cries of astonishment; most thought she was joking. But when she repeated her challenge several times, they realized she was serious. Each of the spinners promised to give up her share of the day's work to O-Katsu, if she went to the waterfall.

"But how will we know if she really goes there?" several women asked.

"Why, let her bring back the money box from the shrine," said the old woman the others had nicknamed "Grandmother." She added, "That will be proof enough. She can return the money in the morning, after she has shown it to us."

"I'll bring it, you'll see," boasted O-Katsu, who did not believe in ghosts. In her greed she had also made up her mind to take the money from the offering box before she returned it.

Bundling a warm robe around her, she hurried out into

the street. The night was frosty but clear. The young woman's wooden clogs made crunching sounds on the ice-crusted road as she hurried down the empty street. All the doors and windows of the houses she passed were shut tight against the piercing cold. But O-Katsu only pulled her robe more tightly about her, and thought of the coins she would take from the shrine in a short while, and the hemp she would take from her fellow workers in the morning.

Soon she left the village behind and hurried along the road that ran between frozen rice fields that glittered in the starlight. For nearly half an hour, she traveled through the great silence. Then she heard the distant roar of the Waterfall of Ghosts.

A little while later she began following a narrow path that wound under high cliffs. Her way grew darker and more dangerous as she neared the bottom, but she had visited the falls before, so she knew the way. The roar of the cascade grew louder and louder.

The path ran around a huge boulder and opened onto a stretch of pebbled shore. The sound of the falls was now deafening; she could see the water like a shining ribbon of silk against the black cliffs. In the starlight she could just make out the curved roof of the shrine and the shadowy square of the money box underneath.

She rushed forward eagerly and stretched out her hand to take it.

But the sound of the waterfall suddenly became a babble of voices crying, "Oh! Wicked woman!"

For a moment O-Katsu stood frozen, gripped with terror.

But she was a bold young woman. "It's only the sound of the water," she said to herself. When she looked at the falls, she seemed to see strange, twisted shapes boiling

about the base. But she told herself, "That's only the mist."

She snatched up the money box and ran.

Behind her the chorus of ghostly voices cried, "Oh! Oh! Oh! Wicked, wicked woman!"

O-Katsu did not stop running until she reached the top of the path. There she paused a moment, gasping for breath. Then she ran back toward the village. Around her, snow began to fall lightly on the ice-covered fields, then faster and faster. A wind rose and tried to push her back the way she had come; in its howling she thought she could hear angry voices crying, "O-Katsu! O-Katsu!"

But she kept on, her robe wrapped snugly around her, and only her eyes uncovered. The snow was drifting so high that even her tall clogs could not keep her feet dry. But she was back in the village now, and she could see the lights of the hemp factory ahead.

Before she went any farther, she took shelter in an alleyway between two buildings and opened the money box. She took all but a handful of copper coins and put these in her kimono. Then she walked toward the lighted windows of the factory.

The other women had all stayed to see if O-Katsu would make good her boast. They cried out in amazement when she entered, panting, with the money box from the shrine.

They brought her to the fire, asking breathless questions about what had happened. O-Katsu told them in a few sentences about hearing ghostly voices—though she did not tell them that the voices had called her "wicked." She said nothing about the coins she had stolen. When the woman nicknamed "Grandmother" opened the box and saw only a few coppers in the bottom, O-Katsu was loudest in crying out how miserly people were to leave such a miserable offering at a shrine.

"How brave you are, O-Katsu," said the young girl whose challenge had started the whole business. "You have certainly earned the hemp we promised."

The others all agreed, and they good-naturedly turned their day's output over to O-Katsu. Then they hurried away to their own homes.

When she was alone, O-Katsu took the stolen coins out of her kimono to count them by the ruddy glow of the fire.

But the offering box, on the floor beside her feet, suddenly began rocking from side to side.

"Oh! What is this?" cried the startled young woman.

As if to answer her, the lid of the box suddenly flew open, and a white mist, like steam, issued from it. O-Katsu looked on in horror, as the mist began to take on strange forms and suddenly became a howling cloud of ghosts. Their bodies were drawn out to amazing lengths; their legs dwindled away to nothingness; their necks were long and twisted like snakes; they stretched their long arms out and clutched at O-Katsu with their thin, pale fingers. Around and around the frightened woman they spun, like a horrible whirlpool, screeching, "Wicked woman! Wicked woman!"

O-Katsu thought she might faint. She sank to her knees and begged the ghosts to leave her alone. Then an idea occurred to her. She took the coins she still held in her hands and returned them to the offering box. When all the money had been put back, the ghosts poured themselves like a waterfall down into the box. The lid closed with a snap.

Quickly dressing in her warm robes, O-Katsu took the box and hurried back to the shrine. There she replaced it, with a promise to give the spirits of that place all the money she would get from selling the hemp she had gained by her disrespectful deed.

This she did the very next morning, and she was never troubled by ghosts again.

The Ghost's Cap

(from a Russian folktale)

In a certain village there was a girl who was as full of mischief as she was lazy. Though her mother and father would nag at her to help with the cooking or mending or sweeping, she would slip away to meet with her friends, who were as useless as she was. They would sit on the banks of the river, gossiping and chattering away, while their mothers washed the clothes and spread them on the bank to dry, near the churchyard.

One day Anya and her friends began talking about who was the boldest. The boasting went on and on, until Anya finally declared, "I'm not afraid of *anything!*"

"Well, then," said one young man, Ivan, "if you're not afraid, go at midnight to the graveyard. My father and uncle say there's a ghost who sits on a tombstone there from the stroke of midnight until the first light of morning. Go, make the ghost tell you its name, and I'll believe that no one is as brave as you. And I'll give you the silver buttons off my jacket that you've admired for so long."

"Oh, *those!*" said the greedy girl, with a toss of her braids. "I'd have to have more than *them* to go to the churchyard at midnight and meet a ghost." In fact she did not believe there was any ghost, because she knew that the young man's father and uncle were notorious for the amount of vodka they drank. They were often seeing spirits in the night, after they'd downed too many glasses of liquor.

"If you'll do it, I'll give you two lengths of lace," said one girl.

"And I'll give you twenty *kopecks,*" offered another girl.

Soon Anya had extracted promises for all sorts of things from her friends. She vowed to go to the graveyard that very night, at the stroke of midnight, and force the ghost to tell her its name.

When she went home that evening, her mother grumbled, "The dust is piling up in the corners of every room, because you won't do your sweeping."

"Soon," said Anya, taking out her favorite embroidered jacket and beginning to cut off the wooden buttons, thinking how grand Ivan's silver ones would look in their stead.

Her father cleared his throat impatiently. "You'd be better off learning to cook a decent meal and do an honest day's work, than worrying about how you look. You'll die a pauper in rags, if you don't have a care."

"Never," said the girl, thinking about the lace and *kopecks* and other things her cleverness would win her this night.

Her parents just threw up their hands and shook their heads at each other.

Shortly before midnight, when her mother and father were asleep, Anya pulled on her shawl and slipped out of the cottage. She planned to walk to the edge of the churchyard, because she was sure some of her friends would be watching from their windows to be sure she was doing what she promised. When she got there, she intended to turn right around and come home. In the morning, she would tell her friends the ghost was the ghost of Old Peter, who had died the spring before. That would satisfy them, and they would have to give her the things they had promised.

So she strolled to the crumbling, low stone wall around the cemetery. She pushed her way through the rusting gate. The full moon shone brightly, filling the place with pale light. Just inside, she saw what looked like a corpse dressed in white from head to foot, sitting on a tombstone.

Anya wasn't the least bit afraid: she thought it was Ivan playing a trick on her. So she ran up to the figure and, pulling the cap off it, shouted, "You won't frighten me!"

The ghostly figure held its peace, never uttering a word. "Are you a ghost waiting for the stroke of midnight to speak?" she teased, "or are you the boy who will have no silver buttons on his jacket in the morning?"

Laughing, she ran back through the moon-splashed streets. When she got home, she looked closer at her prize, and found it was a moldy white cap, half filled with loose earth.

"Ugh!" she cried, tossing it into a dusty corner of her room. Then she blew out the candle and climbed into bed. Three times she came awake, thinking she heard someone tapping at the window. In the rising wind, she thought she heard a voice whispering, "Give me back my cap! Give me back my cap!" But each time she relit the candle and threw open the shutters, she discovered only darkness. Finally she slept soundly until the morning.

The next day she met her friends on the riverbank. She told them she had gone to the churchyard the night before, and two girls admitted they had been spying on her and had indeed seen her walking down the lane toward the cemetery.

"Did you meet the ghost?" asked Ivan.

"To be sure," Anya said, "it's the spirit of Old Peter, who died last spring. He told me so himself. Then I snatched his cap as proof, and here it is."

She held out the dirt-stained cap, enjoying the way her friends shuddered and pulled away from the trophy. Only Ivan stretched out a finger to touch it. Anya tossed it at him, but he jerked away, so it fell onto the grass between them. "Don't you want your cap back," she teased, "since you lost it last night?"

"I've never seen the thing before," said Ivan. Then he reached into his pocket and dropped the silver jacket buttons into Anya's cupped hands.

"You're a liar," she laughed, "but you pay your debts like an honest man." Then she gathered up the rest of her prizes from her friends and hurried back home to hide them away. She paused only long enough to crumple the white cap into a ball and toss it into the river.

The night, long after everyone was asleep, in the hour just before dawn there came an angry tapping at the shutter of Anya's bedroom window. "Give me back my cap!" a voice moaned. But the girl, sleeping heavily and dreaming of silver buttons and lace, never woke up.

But her mother did, and woke Anya's father. They opened the window and saw a ghastly figure in the moonlight.

"What do you want?" asked the mother, trembling.

"My cap, which your daughter stole."

Just at that moment the cocks began to crow, and the ghost disappeared.

Anya's parents woke her up.

"Foolish girl! What have you done?" demanded her father. Then he told her what he and her mother had seen from their window.

"It's only Ivan," said Anya, pulling the bedclothes up around her head. "He's always playing tricks."

Her parents pleaded with her to give back the cap, but she said she had tossed it into the river on her way home, and that was that.

Alarmed, the girl's father and mother sent for the village priest, told him about their horrible visitor, and begged him to help. "You can perform a service to rid us of this ghost, can't you?" they asked.

The priest considered for a while, then told them to bring their daughter to church the next day.

So on the following day, Anya was dragged to church, protesting loudly that she had buttons and lace to sew on her favorite coat. The priest had asked a number of villagers to come to add their prayers to help lay the troubled spirit to rest.

Just as the service was nearly finished, a terrible whirlwind arose. The entire church was shaken, and everyone was hurled to the floor. But Anya was thrown down with even greater force. A single, bloodcurdling scream escaped from her lips. Then everything was silent, and the whirlwind was stilled.

But when the terrified people picked themselves up and looked toward the altar, there on the bottom step, where Anya had been kneeling, was nothing but a single braid of her hair and one silver jacket button.

The Witch Cat

(folklore of the United States—Virginia)

One windy March day back in 1850, a handsome young man, whose wife had died the year before, arrived in a small Virginia town. He brought with him his young daughter, a wagon full of household goods and tools, and enough money to buy a small plot of land.

The townsfolk were kind and showed him several parcels of land that were for sale. Before he decided, he went walking through the back country and found a nice piece of land beside a wide, still pond.

When he asked about it, people said it wasn't owned by anybody. It had once belonged to a family that had left those parts after a string of misfortunes. No one said much, though they tried their best to get him to change his mind. But nothing would do except that land for his farm.

The people in the neighborhood helped him get started. They had a house-raising to build him a cabin and a barn raising the following week. With the last of his money, he bought a horse, a cow, and several chickens.

He worked hard, clearing the land and getting the fields ready for planting. His daughter milked the cow and fed the chickens. They seemed happy enough, though the townsfolk told one another that such a fine man should get married pretty quick, to give himself the sort of companionship a man needs and give his little girl a mother.

Sometimes, when his day's work was done, the farmer would fish for a while on the banks of the pond, staring dreamily out across the waters that turned gold, then red, then purple as the sun set.

One evening, at twilight, he saw a small skiff coming across the water, poled by a tall, slender figure. The glare of the fading sun made it impossible for him to see whether it was a man or a woman on the water.

But when the boat was nearer shore, he saw the stranger was wearing a bonnet. A moment later, as the skiff landed smoothly, a young woman's voice called out, "Hello! Help me up, will you?"

She extended a delicate hand, pale and fine as bone china, to him. Like a man in a dream, the farmer reached out and took it, helping her out of the boat and onto the shore. The woman pulled off her bonnet and shook her curly black hair free. "That feels more to my liking!" she said. "All that rowing can really wear a body out."

For a moment he didn't answer her. He was fascinated by her wide, green eyes, pale skin, and lips as dainty and red as a rosebud. At last he remembered his manners, removed his hat, and said, "Tom Morgan at your service, ma'am. Are you lost?"

"Not a bit!" she said with a laugh. "My name is Eleanor Faye. I live over across the pond." She gestured toward the far side, where willows and cypresses were tangled together. "I figured it was time I called on my new neighbors."

Still in a daze, Tom invited her up to see his cabin and barn, and meet his daughter Effie. Eleanor "ooh'd" and "ah'd" as he pointed out the new house and barn, and the chicken coop with its coat of fresh paint. But when she reached out a hand to stroke Effie's hair, the child, clinging to her father's trouser leg, began to cry, and wouldn't let the woman touch her.

"Shy little thing, isn't she?" said Eleanor with a polite laugh that showed her white teeth. Tom, feeling badly, tried to get his daughter to apologize, but she ran away suddenly.

"I'm sorry about that," said Tom, "she's not usually shy with strangers."

"No matter," said Eleanor easily, "we'll become good friends before long."

It was now nearly dark. "I have to be going," the woman said. "Next time I won't come by so late."

Tom walked her down to the shore. He offered to row her back across the pond, but she said, "No, I've been a widow for five years and doing for myself. I'll manage fine."

It seemed that her pole barely touched the water before the skiff slid quickly and silently toward the shadowed far shore. Tom stood staring for a long time, until he could no longer see Eleanor or her boat in the gathering dark.

After that, Eleanor came almost every day to visit. Once she brought a jar of homemade preserves; another time, it was a lace tablecloth.

Tom was enchanted, but Effie hid if she could get away. If her father forced her to stay inside when Eleanor visited, she sulked in a corner, staying as far away from the smiling woman as possible. Eleanor would blink her green eyes, which seemed flecked with gold, as if she were holding back tears, but she always made a show of excusing the child's actions.

When Effie's father asked her why she acted the way she did, Effie said, "I don't know. I just don't like her, papa."

This bothered Tom a good deal, because he had fallen under the spell of the young woman and was trying to work up nerve enough to ask her to marry him.

He never went across the pond to her farm. She said she preferred to visit him and get away from her chores. And anything she said made sense to him.

In addition to Effie being difficult, Tom was troubled by something getting at his chickens. Night after night, he would be aroused by a blood-curdling cat scream, followed by a fluttering and squawking from the chicken coop. Each time he ran out to see what the matter was, he'd find one or two of his chickens missing, and feathers scattered all around.

Effie had bad dreams of a huge cat with blazing yellow-green eyes, that climbed through the window of her room and curled up on the foot of her bed, waiting for her to go to sleep, so that it could suck the breath of life from her when she did. One morning, Tom found her barely breathing, and there was a round spot in the bedclothes at the foot of her bed, as if something—a cat, maybe—had curled up to sleep there.

When Tom went into town to pick up supplies, the townsfolk took him aside and whispered to him that Eleanor was a witch who lived beside the pond, because it was enchanted, having been sacred to the Indians who had lived there long before the white men had arrived. They also said she had done away with her husband by black magic, though no one was clear how this had been accomplished.

The young farmer refused to believe them. "You're just jealous o' my good fortune," he said.

Folks in town shrugged and went their own way: they knew what they knew.

His daughter got more sickly, and Tom began to fear for her life. Desperate, he went to the neighborhood "conjur man," named Zeke Franklin. The old man was a white witch who helped people, especially those troubled by black magic.

"I can't say for sure who's witchin' you," said Zeke, "but I'll give you somethin' to help."

He got a little bottle, and into it he put a dried snail, a mummified spider, and the toes from the left foot of a tree toad. He added a bit of bat's wing, then corked it, and tied a string around the neck of the bottle.

"That'll do 'er, I reckon," said Zeke. "Next, you take your huntin' knife, whet it as sharp as a briar, and keep it under your piller."

Tom hung the bottle over Effie's bed that night, and from that moment on, she had no more nightmares. But he kept his hunting knife, honed to a razor edge, under his pillow.

In the morning, Eleanor came to visit him, and expressed disgust at the jar Zeke Franklin had given Tom.

"That's foolishness!" she said, sounding downright angry. "I don't have any patience with nonsense like that."

While Tom tried to explain that the "conjur man's" jar had kept Effie from nightmares, Eleanor ran back to her skiff and poled across the pond without ever once looking back at him.

Frantic, Tom shouted after her; but she ignored him. In misery, he returned to his cabin, where Effie hugged him.

That night something got into the chickens again and tore them apart out of sheer meanness.

"I may have lost a lot," Tom said angrily the next morning, "but I'm not gonna lose any more, that's for sure!"

So he sent Effie into town to stay with neighbors. That night, he moved the few remaining chickens into the barn, and hid behind some grain bags near the window.

He hadn't been in hiding long, when he heard the wind rise, followed by a rumble of thunder. A minute later, rain began pounding on the roof shingles, while the wind howled through the cracks in the walls. Tom was a man not easily frightened, but the power of the storm began to make him uneasy. Then he heard a yowl that sent a thrill of terror up his back.

A moment later, he heard a pounding on the doors, as if huge fists were beating upon it. Tom raised himself into a crouch. At the same moment, a monstrous cat with flashing yellow eyes leaped at him through the window of the barn.

The man sliced the air with his knife to defend himself. The briar-sharp blade caught the cat's right paw, severing it completely.

The cat gave a shriek of pain; yellow eyes blazing, it fled back out through the window.

Tom stumbled out of the barn, like a man in a nightmare. A line of red drops led toward the shore; though the rain was washing the trail away, he was able to follow it easily enough.

At the water's edge, he saw the mark of a boat's prow in the mud. Far out, where the rain-pocked lake was lit by flashes of lightning, Tom saw a skiff skimming the black water toward the opposite shore.

He shouted after it, but the wind and thunder drowned out his cries. In a moment he had launched his own boat and was rowing across the storm-lashed pond.

The storm ended shortly before dawn. The neighbors who had care of Effie came to the farm later, when they had begun to wonder why Tom hadn't come to claim his daughter.

Silence lay over the farm. The tracks of a man's boots led down to the shore of the pond, now silver in the late-morning sunlight.

Some brave villagers rowed across the lake at noon. On the far side, they found Tom sprawled lifeless on the muddy shore. Clenched in his fist was the severed paw of a cat.

In the rude cabin farther up the shore, they found Eleanor Faye collapsed face down on the floor. When they turned her over, they found she was dead, and her right hand was gone.

The Green Mist

(a legend from Lincolnshire, England)

In the old days, folk believed that spring came to the world when a Green Mist covered the land and set seeds to bursting and made fields and trees and flowers grow again.

Once there was a family more eager than the rest for the Green Mist to rise and put an end to winter. Their only daughter had grown sickly during the time of cold and snows. She had been the prettiest young woman in the village, but now she was so pale and thin and weak that she could not stand up on her own feet without the help of her parents or one of her brothers.

Everyone else was sure she would die soon enough, but she thought that if she could only see the spring again, she would live. "Oh, mother," she would say over and over again, "if the Green Mist would only come, I'm sure it would make me strong and well, like the trees and the flowers and the corn in the fields."

Her mother promised her that the spring would come soon enough, and she'd grow strong and pretty as ever. But day after day the girl became weaker and more lifeless, like an early-blooming flower when winter comes back after a false spring.

Each morning, they carried her bed to the doorway, so she could watch for the first sign of spring. But the snows lingered and kept the seeds asleep, and the trees leafless, and the fields and flowerbeds locked in its frosty grip.

Finally, in a voice hardly above a whisper, the girl said to her mother, "If the Green Mist doesn't come tomorrow, then I must die. The earth is calling me, and it will cover me soon enough. Oh! If I could only live as long as one of those cowslips that grow by the door each spring, I swear I'd be content!"

"Hush, now, child! Hush!" her mother cautioned. "You don't know who might hear you say such a thing!"

The old woman knew that there were always bogies around—wicked goblins who made mischief and grief for their human neighbors. No one was ever safe; people thought these evil creatures they couldn't see were always spying on them and waiting to play their wretched tricks.

Even as the woman looked nervously around, she thought she heard thin, piping laughter on the icy breeze. And the sound of that merriment came from no one of flesh and bone and blood.

But her worries were quickly forgotten. The next day the Green Mist rose, like an ocean the color of grass in the summer sunshine and as sweet-smelling as the flowers in spring. It covered the countryside, and roused the earth from its winter sleep.

The girl, watching from the doorway, said, "Now, I'll live." She sat in the sun, and laughed with joy, and waved to her father and brothers as they worked in the nearby fields.

She grew stronger and fairer every day that the sun shone; sometimes she would stretch her arms up to it as if she lived by its warmth alone. But when a cloud hid the sun, she suddenly became as pale and wispy as she had been during the long dark winter days and nights.

But there were more sunny days than not, and the cowslips bloomed by the kitchen door. Soon she was running about and laughing like her old self. Every morning she would kneel by the cowslips and water and tend them. Sometimes she would dance for them in the sunshine; sometimes her mother would catch her just staring and staring at the fragant yellow blossoms.

Once, when the old woman leaned down to gather a bouquet of the flowers, the girl cried out, "Oh, mother, don't pick a single one!"

"Why not?" her mother wondered.

"They're pretty enough growing where they are. And I feel that if you plucked a single one, you'd pluck out a bit of my soul with each blossom."

The woman was deeply troubled by these words and the fear she heard in her daughter's voice. She remembered the girl's rash promise that she would be happy living just as long as the cowslips. And she recalled the thin, piping laughter that had followed the girl's words.

Indeed, her child seemed to grow stranger as the cowslips flowered. Yet she also grew more beautiful—and strong enough to do chores around the house or run errands into the village.

One day, in town, she met a handsome young man, who thought her the most beautiful girl he had ever seen. They talked a bit, and he asked if he could come and visit her. She smiled and nodded and told him where she lived.

He came the next day, and they walked together for a long time, hand in hand. In the afternoon, they sat under a tree near the kitchen door; because the day was sunny and warm, the girl fell asleep. While she dreamed, the young

man gathered up the cowslips from beside the kitchen door, and wove these into a wreath. Gently he set it on her head, waking her up.

At first she laughed; but when she pulled the wreath off her head to look at his handiwork, she was horrified to see what he had done.

"You picked the cowslips to make this!" she cried.

"Aye," he said, "a crown of flowers for the prettiest lass in the neighborhood."

But with a moan, she snatched up the wreath and clutched it to her breast. Then she stood staring wildly around at the green trees and sprouting grass and the golden sun and the yellow cowslips most of all. Puzzled, the young man reached for her, but she gave an awful cry, like an animal in pain, and hurried into the house, slamming the door behind her. Nor would she open it when the young man knocked and pleaded with her to tell him what was wrong with his love wreath.

After a time, he gave up calling to her and went sorrowfully back to town.

In the late afternoon, the girl's mother, who had been visiting a neighbor, found her lying on her bed, with the wreath of cowslips in her hand. The old woman put her hand to her mouth to keep from crying out. Then she sat by her child and tried to make her comfortable. But all the day long the girl seemed to fade; nor could her mother coax a single word out of her.

The following morning her family found her lying dead and white and withered, like the shrunken yellow flowers in the wreath still clutched in her hand.

While the old woman clung to her husband and wept, she heard thin, piping laughter through the open window.

Then she knew for a fact that the bogies had heard her daughter's wish. They had let her live as long as the cowslips, but had caused her to fade when the cowslips themselves had died.

The Cegua

(a folktale from Costa Rica)

One evening, a young man from San José, the capital of Costa Rica, rode into a small town north of the city. He was on his way to visit the ranch of a friend situated in a lonely area, but he wasn't sure which road to take out of the town.

He decided to stop in the local *cantina* to quench his thirst and ask directions.

When the proprietor brought him a mug of beer, he told the traveler he still had a fair distance to cover. "But," the proprietor warned, "no one travels these roads after dark. Stay here: I have a room I will let for a few *pesos*—then you can finish your journey in the morning."

The young man shook his head. "I have to reach my friend's ranch tonight."

The older man shook his head. "Only a fool would risk meeting the *Cegua*."

"The *Cegua*!" the traveler exclaimed. "What kind of creature is *that*?"

The *cantina* owner smiled, as if he was unable to believe such ignorance existed. "*Señor,*" he said, "don't folks in

San José know what the *Cegua* is? She is a demon—and heaven keep you from meeting her on the road!"

"I've never heard of such a thing," said the young man. "Bring me another mug of beer, and please explain what you know about this *Cegua*."

When the older man returned with the beer the traveler had ordered, he brought a second mug for himself. He sat down across the rude wooden table and said, "No one who sees the *Cegua* is left with a sound mind. Strong men, in the peak of health, have gone mad from the sight. Some have even died of fright." He began to rattle off the names of locals who had lost their minds or lives because of this monster.

But the younger man interrupted him, saying, "If she is such a terrible devil, why haven't I heard of her before?"

"She prefers certain parts of our country; we have the misfortune to be one such place," explained the proprietor patiently. "For that reason, no one here rides alone after dark. If someone must travel after nightfall, he always goes with a companion."

"Why? Doesn't she like crowds?" laughed the young man, who was beginning to feel the effects of his long ride and the beer.

"The *Cegua* only appears to someone who travels alone," said the older man gravely, finishing his own beer and starting to rise. "She appears as a beautiful *señorita,* smiling sadly and fluttering her eyes, pleading for a ride—but woe to the traveler who stops to help her! If the unsuspecting rider sits her in front, she turns her head. If he has placed her behind him, she will make him turn to look at her. In either case, his doom is sealed."

"How so?" the traveler asked.

"When he looks, the beautiful *señorita* is gone. The creature riding with him has a huge horse's head, with monstrous fangs. Her eyes burn fiery red, like hot coals, and her breath stinks like sulfur. With a hiss, she will bury her claws in the shoulders of the rider and hang on like a wild animal. A horse, sensing that he is being ridden by a demon, will bolt in such a frenzy that no one can stop him."

"What then?" asked the younger man, no longer smiling quite so broadly.

"Those who are found the next day, if they are still alive, will have gone mad from the sight of her."

"Nonsense," said the traveler, suddenly standing up and tossing down a few *pesos* to pay for the beer. "I must be on my way, if I'm to reach my friend's ranch tonight."

The older man shrugged, gathered up the coins, and turned away. Clearly, he thought to himself, there is no arguing with a fool.

The little town square was deserted. The traveler untied his horse from the hitching post and set out along the road the *cantina*'s proprietor had pointed out to him earlier.

It was a warm night. Not a breath of wind stirred the leaves in the trees on either side of the road. Nothing disturbed the silence, except the *clop-clop* of his horse's hoofs on stones in the roadway.

Suddenly, around a bend, when the town was out of sight behind him and no other building was visible, he saw a slender figure standing in the thick shadows where the trees overhung the road.

Slowing his horse, the young man discovered a beautiful girl, with a pale face framed by the black-lace *mantilla* that covered her head, and which she held under her chin with her left hand. In the moonlight he could see she had curly black hair, huge dark eyes, and deep red lips.

"*Señor,*" she began. Her voice was sweet, but so weak and

weary that he feared she must be near fainting. "I am so tired, but I must go to see my mother, who is ill. Would you take me to Bagaces?"

"Of course," he said, bringing his horse to a stop and climbing down. Bowing slightly and removing his hat, he said, "My friend's ranch is just south of that town. You can spend the night there. In the morning I will escort you the rest of the way."

"You are very kind, *señor*," she said, in such a faint whisper that he had to lean close to make out her words. Then he helped her onto the horse—which had grown restive during their halt—behind his saddle. He mounted himself, and they took off at a good trot.

A breeze had arisen to freshen the still air and flutter the leaves on the nearby trees. The moon and stars tinted the landscape pale silver. Several times the traveler tried to make conversation with the woman, but she didn't answer. She only leaned her head against his back and clung to his shoulders with her hands, as if she were afraid of fainting and tumbling from the horse.

Abruptly his horse, without any prodding, broke into a gallop. The woman dug her fingers into his shoulder, clearly afraid of falling. The young man was too polite to tell her that her nails were digging into his skin.

The horse gave a cry and charged down the dark road as though something terrible were pursuing them. The traveler pulled back on the reins and shouted, but it did no good. His horse only galloped faster.

Suddenly he felt razor-sharp teeth lock onto his neck so that only the collar of his coat saved his skin. An instant later, he heard a cry that came from no human throat as the awful teeth suddenly pulled away a mouthful of his coat collar.

He wrapped the ends of the reins around the fingers of

one hand, and with his free hand he struggled to pry loose the fingers that were clamped on his shoulder. As shadow, then moonlight, then shadow again, washed over the horse and its two riders, the young man saw that the fingers clutching him were too pale—they were the white of bone, rather than fair skin.

He heard another screech and smelled the creature's foul breath. He felt his strength giving out, while the bony fingers pulling at him seemed to grow stronger. The jaws snapped at the back of his neck, this time drawing blood.

Then, ahead, he could see his friend's ranch. He thought he could hear dogs barking, to signal his arrival. Lights were burning in the *hacienda*. There were figures running up the road toward him, carrying torches.

There was a final, ear-splitting scream from the demon behind him. He felt his whole body jerked backward. The hand that was tangled in the reins pulled backward suddenly, causing his horse to rear up, then fall sideways. Both riders fell with the animal.

The traveler was knocked senseless for a moment. When he came to, his friend, holding a torch, was staring at him, asking if he was all right. He nodded, still shaking from his near-brush with death. When he touched his hand to the stinging at the back of his neck, his fingers came away bloody. He looked around hastily, but all he saw was a crowd of friendly-looking *campesinos,* countrymen, watching him. One was calming his horse, which was on its feet again.

"Where is it—the creature?" he asked his friend.

"What creature?"

"The *Cegua.*"

"My friend," laughed the other man, "you stayed too long at some *cantina,* I think. The *Cegua* is a story to frighten children, nothing more. Still, next time you ride at night, be sure you travel with a companion. These lonely roads can be dangerous in the dark."

The young man said nothing, but he shivered just a little when the night breeze brought the lingering odor of sulfur to his nostrils.

The Ghostly Little Girl

(United States—California)

Near the turn of the century, in the seacoast town of Monterey, California, lived a widowed fisherman, Richard Colter, and his young daughter, Maria. Their home was a weather-beaten shack of boards with a tin roof, on the shore some distance from town.

Maria Colter was a pretty, but strong-willed little girl. Her father worked hard, fishing for sardines, salmon, cod, tuna, and yellowtail in Monterey Bay and the Pacific Ocean, just beyond, so that Maria could go to the Catholic school in town. She was very popular with the other girls who were pupils there, though a few parents did not approve of someone whose father was so poor.

Maria's closest friends were Annie Kelly, Susan Cooke, and Catherine Hopper.

In the early spring, Maria was absent from school for several days. Her three friends asked their teachers about it, but were told only that Maria and her father had sailed out of Monterey Bay three days before. Their boat had last been seen by another fisherman, around noon, beyond Point Lobos.

"But I *saw* her this morning, on my way to school,"

Annie Kelly told Susan Cooke and Catherine Hopper. "She was standing across the street, watching me. I waved to her, but she didn't wave back. I don't think she saw me, because she ran away right after that. I didn't see her again."

But once again Maria's desk at school was empty. As her three friends walked home, they talked about her absence.

"Maybe her father is sick, and she has to take care of him," Annie suggested.

"Maybe she got sick herself," Susan said. "Maybe she was starting to come to school today, and had to go home."

"I think we should go and see what's happened to her," said Catherine decisively.

The girls knew their friend lived with her father in a shanty outside of Monterey. They decided to pay a visit as soon as school was over. But it was a long walk, and they took their time, poking along the beach.

It was very late in the day, when, far down along the shore, they could see a single cabin, the back of which was built on stilts that extended down into the water.

"I'll bet that's Maria's house," said Annie.

"I hope so," said Susan, "because it's getting pretty late. I'll be in trouble if I don't get home by supper."

"Maybe we shouldn't go," said Annie. "I don't see any lights."

"Don't be silly!" said Catherine impatiently. "We've come this far."

"But it *is* getting awfully late," added Susan.

"I just want to see how Maria is. Then we can go right home."

But by the time they reached the run-down shack, a thick, wet evening fog had crept in, heavy with the tang of salt. Walking softly and whispering to each other, the three friends climbed the stairs to the rickety front porch. It was piled high with rotting fishing nets, rusted crabbing cages, buckets, and odd bits of rope and canvas. Around the corner of the house they could see a little pier, but no boat was tied to it. Everything was quiet except for the roar of waves hitting the shore.

"I don't think there's anyone home—let's go!" urged Annie, as the haunting call of a seagull cut through the foggy air. The mist was swirling so thickly around them that they could no longer see the distant roofs of Monterey. Tentacles of fog were tangling in the live oaks and pines far up the hillside.

"Don't be a ninny!" hissed Catherine. Boldly she knocked one-two-three times on the door. When there was no response, she pounded on the door even louder.

"Let's look through a window," suggested Susan.

This seemed a good idea, since clearly no one was coming to answer the door. Tiptoeing to the nearest window, the girls peeked in past ragged curtains.

At first all they saw was an empty room, with a few sad pieces of furniture scattered around. An unlit kerosene lantern stood in the middle of a wooden table. Opposite the window was a single closed door.

Suddenly a strange glow began to seep under the closed door. Then the door opened slowly, and they could see Maria Colter framed in the glow of the unearthly light. She was standing upright, but her eyes were closed, as if she were in a deep sleep.

Without a sound, the girl, like a sleepwalker, crossed the room. A moment later the three friends on the porch heard the cabin's front door unlocked with a loud *click,* then pulled open with a squeal, because the damp had swollen the wood.

Annie, Susan, and Catherine looked at one another for a moment. Then they went to the open door and peered through. The room inside was empty again, with only a faint silver-gray light coming through the streaked windows. The door in the far wall was closed, though they could still see the line of curious light underneath it.

Their friend had vanished.

"She must have gone back into that other room," said Susan.

"Why is she playing tricks on us?" asked Annie, "I don't think we should stay here anymore."

But Catherine walked bravely into the room and yelled, "Maria! We just want to say hello! You can come out." She was reaching for the knob of the closed door when something stopped her. There was a smell of saltwater so strong that they could almost taste the salt. The odor of fish was strong enough to make Susan hold her nose. The roar of the ocean filled the room as though it was circling the house outside.

"Catherine," Annie said, her voice little more than a squeak, "Look! The door!"

Water was beginning to seep under the door, soaking the worn carpet. The three girls stepped back, afraid to let it touch their shoes.

Abruptly they were startled by a crash like a huge wave hitting the other side of the door. It amazed them that the door didn't splinter from the impact. A moment later a second blow shuddered the door.

The three friends just gaped, too frightened to move. In the silence that followed, broken only by the gurgle of the water still seeping out under the door, they heard a ghostly voice from the other side of the door. It sounded like someone calling from underwater.

"Catherine!" it called. "Annie! Susan! I *knew* you'd come looking for me. I'll be with you in just a minute!"

There was a last *boom* against the door; then a deep silence fell over the room that smelled of fish and salt and seaweed.

The door began to open. There was silver light all around it. The puddle of water on the floor looked like a tide pool in the moonlight. They saw a little girl's hand, pale as whitefish, wet, and wrinkled as something that has lain in the water too long.

Terrified, the three girls ran from the shack as fast as they could, out into the thick, wet fog. They didn't stop running until they were back in their own neighborhood. There, while they caught their breath, they tried to make some sense of their frightening experience. Had Maria been playing a trick on them? If so, why? But that didn't explain the strange light and the sound and smell of the ocean inside the house or the crash of waves against the closed door.

Finally, confused and frightened, the girls decided to tell their parents what they had seen.

It was Catherine's father who told them, "Richard Colter's boat sank three days ago. They found his body washed ashore near Point Lobos. His little girl, Maria, drowned with him, but they haven't found her body yet."

The Midnight Mass of the Dead

(a Norse folktale)

There was once a very devout widow who lived in a small village in Norway and went to church every day. For many years Juliana would go with her friend Berta to these services. When Berta died, she went alone.

One Christmas Eve, she thought she would go to the early service on Christmas morning. Since there were fewer people at this mass, she could sit nearer the altar, feeling close to the Christ child on this holiest of days.

Before she went to bed Christmas Eve, she put out coffee, so she could have something warm to drink because she did not want to go to church on an empty stomach.

Juliana's alarm failed to wake her, but she roused herself out of a deep sleep sometime Christmas morning. Moonlight was streaming through onto the bedroom floor when she got up. She looked at her little alarm clock, but it had stopped with the hands frozen at eleven-thirty. She did not know for sure *what* time it was, so she went over to the window and looked down the street to the church. Light was shining through all the windows; and, opening her window sash for a moment, she was sure she could hear singing carried to her ears on the chill breeze.

She hastily set the coffee boiling while she dressed. She downed a cup of the strong, black brew, then got out her long, pink cloth coat, lined and trimmed with rabbit fur, which she only wore on special occasions. Tying a white scarf around her head and gathering up her prayer book, she set out for the church.

Oddly enough it was very quiet on the street, and she did not see a soul on the way. Usually Christmas morning brought many to even the earliest services—souls who might otherwise never go to worship during the year.

When she entered the church, she found a pew very near the altar. But when she glanced around, it seemed to her that all the other people looked pale and strange, though she was not rude enough to stare at them. The woman on her right had deep circles around her eyes, as though she had just gotten over some terrible illness; the man on her left clutched the back of the pew in front of him with fingers so long and thin, they hardly seemed to have any flesh on them at all. It seemed to Juliana that there wasn't anyone kneeling around her that she knew—yet, she had the feeling she had met many of them before, though she could not say where or when.

She settled back into the hard wooden pew along with the rest of the congregation, when the pastor left the altar and climbed half a dozen short steps up to the pulpit. He was not Pastor Solvold, nor any of the city ministers she was familiar with. The visitor was a tall, pale man who preached quite well. Again she had the nagging feeling that she knew him from sometime long ago, but she could not place him.

He spoke of death and those who lay waiting the resurrection under the Christmas snows and who grew impatient with eternity. Juliana found his themes morbid and not at all the message of joy and hope she expected. The preacher rambled on, and she became restless, shifting uncomfortably in her pew. As she let her mind wander, she realized there was not the noise and coughing and throat clearing that she was used to hearing at any early mass. The silence was so absolute that when she nervously dropped her prayerbook, the sound seemed to boom out from the altar to the choir loft. The preacher paused and stared at her with red-rimmed eyes that had no trace of kindness in them at all.

Juliana picked up her prayerbook, but she was feeling so uneasy that her hand was trembling.

When the preacher had finished his sermon, he led the congregation in a hymn. The music was strange, and the words were unfamiliar to Juliana.

"Leaves have their time to fall,
    And flowers wither at the northwind's breath,
    And stars to set—but all,
    Thou hast *all* seasons for thine own, O Death!"

She was so uncomfortable that she could not get any words out. She was aware of the woman on her right and the man on her left staring at her with the same intensity as had the strange pastor.

Suddenly while the singing continued, a woman who was sitting behind Juliana leaned forward and whispered in her ear, "Throw your coat over your shoulders and go quickly! If you're still here when the mass is over, you're finished! This is a service held by the Dead."

Now the widow was so frightened, she wasn't sure her legs would support her. But she recognized the voice of the woman who had warned her, and turned around.

It was Berta, her friend, who had died many years ago. In a flash, she realized that the pastor and other members of the congregation that she had recognized were persons who had died in the parish over the years. She shivered from terror; but Berta gave her shoulder a reassuring squeeze, so she pulled her coat loosely around her and got up to leave.

But just as she reached the aisle, the woman with the sunken eyes and the man with the bony fingers began to screech. These ghastly figures turned in the pew and snatched at her.

Like a sea that has suddenly been churned by winds, the crowd of horrible, pale churchgoers rose in their pews and began clamoring toward the aisle. They yelled and moaned and scratched at her, their hands like claws, with dirt and mold beneath their cracked, yellow fingernails.

Sobbing "No, no, no," Juliana pushed her way down the aisle. Just as she shoved her way through the doors and out onto the church steps, she felt her coat pulled from her shoulders by the creatures chasing her. Without giving it a second thought, she let them have the coat, and ran down the steps into the windy street beyond.

The moment she reached her own door, she heard a clock somewhere chiming one. She fumbled out her key, unlatched the door, and slammed it behind her. Half dead with terror, she set about lighting every lamp and candle in her room. Then she sat on the couch, determined to keep watch through the small hours of the night. But exhausted as she was, she fell asleep.

Juliana awoke late in the morning. Most of the candles had burned themselves out; only a single lamp was still burning on the mantle. Through the gray light, she heard the church summoning the faithful to Christmas morning services.

Had she dreamed it all? she wondered.

But when she went to put on her favorite coat, she could not find it in the closet. Putting on an old black coat, she went out into the street and was greeted by her neighbors, who were hurrying to mass. Yes, she told herself, it had all been a nightmare, and she had simply misplaced her coat. She would find it soon enough.

She had to force herself to mount the steps and enter the back of the church, for all that it was crowded with friends and neighbors. But she turned and fled when the sexton came up to her, saying, "I think this is yours, isn't it? I've seen you wearing it at church before."

He held out to Juliana her pink cloth coat, with the rabbit lining and trim, that had been torn into a thousand strips.

Tailypo

(United States—West Virginia)

Not so very long ago, an old man lived by himself in the backwoods of West Virginia. He had a log cabin with a single room that held a stove, a bed, a table, a chair, and a big open fireplace built of fieldstone.

One night the man sat eating a plateful of beans and bread and regretting that he hadn't been able to catch a single fish in the lake behind his cabin or bag a single possum or deer for his supper. He was startled to look across the table and see the strangest creature he had ever seen, sitting on its haunches in the far corner of the room, staring at him.

It had jaws like a weasel, ears like a fox, piercing yellow eyes like an owl, a monkey's body, and was covered in bright red fur. But mainly it had a huge, long tail that coiled around and around it, the way a rattler coils on itself before it strikes.

"What th—!" cried the man. "How'd you get in here?" He grabbed his carving knife from beside the loaf of bread and went after the animal. The thing gave a screech like nothing the man had heard before; then it scrambled out through a chink between two of the cabin's logs.

But it wasn't quick enough. With a single slice, the man cut the creature's tail off, while the rest of the animal scampered away to the woods. The man walked back to the table and stretched out the tail, marveling at its length. After a few minutes he decided that meat was meat, and that was what he was hungry for right now.

So he cooked up that tail, found it tasted a little like rabbit, and ate it all at one sitting. After that, he plugged up the hole between the logs, went to bed, and soon was fast asleep.

He hadn't been asleep very long when he heard something scratching at the door, just like a cat. Pretty soon, he heard it call, "Tailypo, tailypo; just give me my tailypo."

Now he had three dogs that slept under the house. He whistled for them, and they came charging out and chased the creature far into the woods. But only two of his dogs came back. When the man saw this, he cursed a blue streak. Then he sent the dogs to sleep under the floorboards and went back to bed himself.

A short time later, he heard the same clawing at the front door, as the creature tried to get in. Then he heard it call through a crack in the door, "Tailypo, tailypo; just give me my tailypo."

Once again the man whistled up his dogs from underneath the cabin, and they chased the creature all the way down the road, snapping so close behind that if it had still had a tail, it would have lost it to the hounds.

The man heard the dogs giving chase until the woods swallowed up the sound. But a little later only one dog returned.

Again the man cursed loudly. This time he had his remaining dog sleep at the foot of his bed.

In the smallest hours of the morning, he heard something scrabbling at the window, like a night bird trying to

get in. Through the cracked glass he heard, "Tailypo, tailypo; I've got to have my tailypo."

Quick as he could, he flung the cabin door open and sent his last dog out into the night. He heard the dog charging around the corner of the cabin and heard the creature screeching and scrambling away.

After that, things were pretty quiet. But the last hound never did return.

The man stayed awake a long time, listening, but he heard nothing more. Finally, just before dawn, he fell asleep. But he woke up a few minutes later. He was sure he'd heard something in his room. He looked into the far corner and saw the patch he'd put over the hole was gone. Then he heard something scrabbling up the foot of his bed. A minute later he saw a fox's ears, a weasel's jaws, and two huge yellow eyes—just like an owl's—looking at him.

He tried calling for his dogs, but they were gone. He was too frightened to climb out of bed. He just kept staring while the red, monkeylike creature crept closer, and closer—

"Tailypo, tailypo," it growled, "just give me my tailypo."

"But-but-but," the man stuttered, "I haven't got your tailypo."

Then the horrible creature which was by then sitting on the man's knees, snarled and said, *"Oh, yes, you have!"*

And it jumped on the man's chest and scratched him all to pieces.

There are those who say that the creature got its tailypo back, and some who say it didn't. But the fact is, that old man and his dogs were never seen again in West Virginia or anywhere else.

Lady Eleanore's Mantle

(from a tale by Nathaniel Hawthorne)

When America was still a British colony, a young woman, Lady Eleanore Rochcliffe, traveled from England to become the ward of Governor Shute of Massachusetts Bay. The gentleman and his wife were Eleanore's only surviving relatives, and very happy to have her stay in Province House, the governor's home in Boston.

Lady Eleanore was beautiful, witty, well-educated, and extremely proud of her place in the world. She wanted nothing to do with anyone who was not as highborn and rich as herself. She was not at all sure that the colonies had much to offer her, after life in London at the royal court.

But she was quite impressed when the governor sent an elegant coach, drawn by four sleek black horses, to meet her ship and carry her to Province House. He also arranged for a gallant escort of gentlemen on horseback to ride before and behind her coach.

People in the street glimpsed Lady Eleanore through the large glass windows of the coach and thought she looked very much like a queen—though she was still in her teens. But what caused the most comment was her embroidered mantle, which had been woven by the most skillful seamstress in London. Its gold, silver, and red threads seemed to catch fire from the late-afternoon sun so that the young woman appeared wrapped in a cloak of flames.

When the coachman reined in his four black steeds in front of Province House, a nearby church bell tolled for a funeral. Everyone was upset that its mournful *clang* accompanied Lady Eleanore's arrival.

Just then, as Governor Shute and his wife approached the carriage to assist their ward in climbing down, a pale young man with tangled hair rushed from the crowd and fell in the dust at Eleanore's feet, offering his back as her footstool.

"Get up, sir!" roared the governor, threatening to beat the young man with his cane.

"Don't strike him," said Eleanore scornfully. "When men want to be trampled on, I am happy to give them the favor they deserve."

Light as a sunbeam on a cloud, she placed her foot upon the waiting back, extended her hand to meet that of the governor, and stepped down.

"Who is this insolent fellow?" the governor's wife demanded.

"Gervase Helwyse," replied the governor's doctor, "a youth without position or fortune, but of good mind—until he met Lady Eleanore in London. He fell in love with her, but she would have nothing to do with anyone in such humble circumstances. Her scorn drove him mad."

"He was mad even to dream of approaching so noble a lady as my ward," said the governor, signaling the discussion was at an end.

A few days after this incident, a ball was given in honor of Lady Eleanore's arrival. Province House was filled with the richest and most noteworthy gentry in Boston. The ladies shone in rich silks and satins, spread out over wide hoops; the gentlemen glittered with gold embroidery laid unsparingly on the purple, or scarlet, or sky-blue velvet of their coats and waistcoats. The place was alive with voices, laughter, and music.

But no person drew the eye and admiration of the crowd like Lady Eleanore. And her mantle gave an added majesty and mystery to her. The story went around that it had been made by a dying girl and had the magic power of giving new grace and beauty to the wearer every time it was put on. It was said that the fanciful birds and animals and flowers that adorned it were the product of a mind grown delirious with approaching death.

To some of those looking at the young woman, it seemed that the strange magic of the mantle gave her an almost feverish flush, while others thought it made her skin look as pale as the most delicate bone china. Eleanore herself seemed as changeable: sometimes she chattered and laughed excitedly with certain select guests; just as often she seemed moody and withdrawn and tired to the point of fainting.

While the guests were taking refreshment, Lady Eleanore settled into a large damask chair with a sigh, chatting with the governor's doctor, who noted her sudden weariness with a professional eye.

Suddenly Gervase Helwyse appeared, kneeling at her feet, having slipped unnoticed through a side door. "I beg you, dear lady, throw off that mantle," he cried. "It may not be too late! Throw the accursed thing in the fire!"

But Lady Eleanore, with a scornful laugh, drew the rich folds of the embroidered mantle around her head, so that it threw her features half into shadow and gave her a mysterious look. "Leave me," she mocked. "But always remember me as you see me now!"

At this, he was dragged from the room by the doctor and several other gentlemen and servants, who shoved him roughly out the iron gate of Province House and slammed it shut with a loud *clang*.

As the night wore on, the weariness in Eleanore's manner increased; her face grew flushed; she smiled because it seemed too much effort to speak. The doctor whispered something in the governor's ear that changed the man's cheerful expression to one of fear and worry. A few moments later it was announced that unforeseen circumstances made it necessary to end the party immediately. Puzzled, the guests went home.

The curious events at the ball were quickly forgotten, when, a few days later, the city was thrown into a panic by an outbreak of smallpox, which in those days could not be prevented or cured. At first the disease struck only the proud, the well-born, and the wealthy, though it soon spread throughout the whole city and countryside.

It was pointed out that the first to fall victim were persons who had attended Lady Eleanore's ball at Province House. In fact, the blood-red flag that marked every house where smallpox had entered, had first been seen waving over the door of Province House.

Though no one outside the house had seen Lady Eleanore since the night of the ill-fated ball, it was rumored that the disease had crossed the sea from London in her gorgeous mantle. It was said that fate and misery had been woven into its gold and silver threads by a woman already dying of the disease. People whispered that this had been a punishment of Eleanore for her pride and cruelty.

People cursed her and called each red warning flag, "A new triumph for the Lady Eleanore."

They shunned Province House, and most of its inhabitants fled. So there was no one to stop Gervase Helwyse when he entered one evening. Quickly he climbed the stairs to the upper hallway, throwing open door after door, calling "Lady Eleanore!"

At last, from the gloom of a darkened chamber, a woman's voice murmured, "A drop of water! My throat is scorched!"

Gervase stepped a little way into the room. Spotting the mantle, into which a dead woman had innocently embroidered a spell of dreadful power, he shuddered. Then he drew near the canopied bed, where something stirred behind the silken curtains. He pulled the drapes apart and saw a skeletal figure that tried to hide a hideous face with clawlike hands. "Do not look at me!" the woman croaked.

"Who are you?" asked the young man, fascinated and repelled by the vision. "What are you doing in my lady's chamber?"

"I am one who wrapped myself in pride as in a mantle and scorned you," she rasped, "Now you are avenged. I am Eleanore Rochcliffe."

"Another triumph for the Lady Eleanore!" cried Gervase, driven completely mad by her words. "All have been her victims! It is fitting that the final victim is herself!"

Then, laughing wildly, he snatched up the fatal mantle and ran from Province House.

That night a torchlit procession, led by Gervase, carried the straw figure of a woman, wrapped in a fantastically embroidered mantle, to the square in front of Province House. There the mob burned the effigy, and a strong wind came and swept away the ashes. And it was said from that hour, the disease abated, as if, from first to last, it had some mysterious connection with Lady Eleanore's mantle.

No one knew the lady's fate for certain. But for a long

time afterward, there was talk that in a certain chamber of the mansion, a woman's ghostly form could be seen, shrinking into the shadows and muffling her face with a richly embroidered mantle.

The Soldier and the Vampire

(a Russian folktale)

In the days when the czars still ruled Russia, a soldier was allowed to go home on leave to attend the wedding of his sister. He traveled on foot; and though it was a long journey, it was a pleasant one. It was almost summer, and the days were mild; the countryside he crossed was thick with forests and sweeping meadows filled with wildflowers. He was eager to see his family after his long absence, so he set himself a "double-time" march pace and whistled a lively tune as he hurried along.

Late in the day he came to a mill less than two hours from the village where he had been born. It belonged to an old friend, so he stopped there to beg something to eat and drink, because he had had nothing to eat since morning.

The miller welcomed him warmly and set out a generous meal for the younger man. Soon the two of them were chattering away about this and that.

Suddenly the soldier looked through the window at the darkening sky and cried, "It's almost nightfall. I'll have to make haste the rest of the way home." He started to get up from the table.

"Spend the night here, my friend!" said the miller quickly. "It's so late, you're sure to run into trouble."

"What do you mean?" the younger man asked.

"A terrible wizard died near the village recently," his friend explained. "Every night he rises from his grave as a vampire, wanders the countryside, and steals the lives of the innocent to prolong his own life-in-death. Even a brave soldier like you should be afraid of such an evil creature."

"I've seen evil enough in war," said the soldier gently. "Meeting a monster such as you describe can't seem too bad after the horrors of the battlefield. And I'm eager to see my family as soon as possible."

The miller tried to argue further with him, but the young man's mind was made up. So off he went.

As it turned out, he reached the village without seeing the vampire. But when he reached his parents' cottage, he heard lamenting and weeping coming from inside. Pushing open the door, he found his parents and the young man who was to become his brother-in-law huddled by the fire, trying to comfort each other.

"Oh, my son!" cried his mother, rushing to embrace the soldier, "you've come for a wedding, but you'll go to a funeral instead." She began sobbing against his chest.

His father placed a hand sadly on the young man's shoulder and told him, "Tonight we discovered your sister had been visited by a wizard who has risen from the grave and who plagues us. She sleeps the sleep that will end in death tomorrow night, when the creature uses her life to escape his grave once more. And there is nothing to be done."

"Why haven't you destroyed the body of this vampire before now?" demanded the soldier, distraught at the news.

"No one knows where the creature lies buried during the

day," the young man who was to marry his sister explained. "And at night he is too powerful to resist."

At this the soldier went into the back room. His sister, dressed as a bride, lay on her bed, pale in the moonlight streaming through a single narrow window. Her chest barely rose and fell; she seemed to grow weaker with each breath she drew. Her hands, palms open at her sides, showed red wounds where something had pierced them and drawn off some of her blood.

The soldier left the room quietly and walked to the door of the cottage.

"Where are you going?" his father asked.

"To try and undo the horror that's been done tonight," answered the soldier. Then he marched out into the darkness, before they could draw him back inside.

He walked the road that ran past the village graveyard but met no one. He was almost a half mile beyond it, where the road ran through a thick part of the forest, when a dark figure, smelling of damp and earth, came shambling out of the shadows. The figure fell in step beside him, but the soldier kept walking along, as if he hadn't a fear in the world, though he guessed it was the wizard returned from the dead who was keeping pace with him.

Now the soldier's travels had taken him far and wide, and shown him many things, so he was able to make a sign with his right hand that signaled to the wizard that he was a wizard also.

"Hail, brother," said the shadowy figure, "what are you doing here?"

"I heard that you have found the secret of life-in-death," said the young man boldly, "and that by stealing some of the blood of the living, you are able to cheat death for another day."

"That's true enough," confessed the wizard. "Only to-night I stole the lifeblood of a village maiden. Tomorrow, at sunset, her life will become mine, and she will die so that I can live."

"How is this done?" asked the soldier.

"Come with me, and I will show you," said the wizard. "But I feel the dawn is drawing near, and I must return to my grave before light. You can keep me company on my way."

Together they turned off the path and entered the shadowy woods. For a long time they made their way through the tangled trees and bushes in silence. At last they entered a clearing, where just enough moonlight sifted through the branches to let the soldier see the face of the wizard, which was streaked with dirt and mold. In the center of the open space, the earth lay tumbled about, and the young man guessed this was the sorcerer's grave.

Seating himself on a fallen log, the soldier said, "Now, make good your promise, and tell me the secret of life-in-death."

From the pocket of his rotting waistcoat, the wizard took a small flask of blood. It glowed like fire in the moonlight. "Just before dawn, I will swallow this. Then the girl's life will leave her body and enter mine the following sunset."

"And if those few drops of blood were returned to her, would she awake?"

Smiling, the wizard shook his head. "If I was destroyed utterly, so that not a bit of my soul escaped, then she would be restored. My magic is already at work on her. And now," said the monster, taking a step toward the soldier, "I'll tear you to pieces. Though you know a thing or two, you're no true wizard to be asking me these questions."

Then the soldier realized that the wicked creature had only been toying with him, luring him into the woods to destroy him and maybe steal his life, too.

"In God's name, I won't give you an easy time of it!" cried the soldier, jumping up and drawing his sword.

The wizard gnashed his teeth and howled like a wolf at mention of the holy name and the sight of cold steel, which is one thing such creatures fear. The soldier began swinging his blade wildly. The wizard, who kept leaping from one side to the next, tried to grab hold of the young man with his clawlike hands.

Finally, after they had fought almost to a standstill, the vampire struck the soldier's sword arm and sent his blade flying away into the shadows. Instantly the creature fell on the young man, who struggled and struggled, but felt his strength giving out. "Ah!" he thought to himself, "I'm done for now."

But at that instant the cocks began to crow, and the first light of dawn touched the tips of the tallest trees. The vampire fell lifeless to the ground.

Quickly the soldier took the flask of blood from the creature's pocket. Then he built a pyre of aspen boughs, placed the wizard's body on it, and set it on fire. He drew his sword and circled the edge of the flames.

As the fire grew hotter, the body changed to a mass of snakes, lizards, toads, worms, and beetles. These tried to creep away from the blaze. But the soldier remembered he had to destroy the creature utterly, so not a bit of his wicked soul could escape. He caught each crawling thing and flung it back into the fire, so that not the tiniest insect escaped.

When the body was utterly consumed, he scattered the ashes to the four winds. Then he returned to the village, where he poured the stolen drops of blood back into the wounds in his sister's hands, so that she came awake again.

After that, the wedding went on as planned. And the village was never troubled by the vampire again.

The Skeleton's Dance

(a folktale from Japan)

In Japan, many years ago, there were two young men, Taro and Jiro, who were good friends. When they were old enough, they left the village in which they had been born to journey together to the distant city to make their fortunes.

Now Taro worked very hard and earned a great deal of money. But Jiro quickly fell in with companions of the wrong sort and spent all his time lounging in tea shops during the day, becoming drunk and roisterous at night, and learning the ways of thieves and murderers.

Still, the young men remained friends, though Taro was very sad to see how corrupt Jiro had become. After three years, Taro decided to return home and asked his friend to join him. It was his hope that, away from the city and its wicked ways, Jiro might become again the good man he had once seemed.

In truth, Jiro had borrowed and spent a great deal of money, and many of his former companions were demanding he pay them back. He was eager to escape the city, because he had no intention of making good his debts. So he said to Taro, "I really do want to go back, but I have no clothes for the trip."

Since he now had a good deal of money, Taro happily shared it with his friend. He gave Jiro money enough for clothes and some extra to buy food and lodging along the way. However, when they reached the mountain pass, beyond which lay their home village, Jiro attacked Taro and killed his friend. He took Taro's money, rolled the body beneath a bush, and went the rest of the way home, as if nothing had happened.

The villagers greeted him warmly, and many asked, "What has become of your good friend, Taro."

"Oh," replied Jiro, "that is a sad story. He fell in with bad companions the moment we reached the city. From that day to this, he has done nothing but waste his money in the company of the most wicked men. I begged him to return with me, in the hopes that he would mend his ways once he was home. But he only laughed at me, and made rude remarks about this village, and had his criminal friends drive me away."

At this, there was much indignant head shaking among the villagers, who said that Taro deserved whatever misery happened to him.

For a few days Jiro made a show of being the same good-hearted fellow he had once been. But he quickly began to gamble and waste his money in drunken revels. Soon he had spent all the money he had stolen from Taro. Because he refused to do honest work, he decided to return to the city, where he would give himself another name and live by stealing from wealthy citizens.

On his way back, he again traveled the mountain pass, where he had killed his friend, Taro. As he was striding through the pass, he heard a voice calling, "Jiro! Jiro!"

Puzzled, he looked all around, but could see nothing

except bushes and the rocky mountain walls. Thinking the wind was playing a trick on him, he continued on his way.

But he had only gone a few paces when the voice cried again, "Jiro! Jiro!"

Determined to find the answer to this mystery, he followed the cries to a thicket far back from the road. Parting the brush and peering through, Jiro discovered a skeleton sprawled on the ground. Even as he looked on in amazement, the skeleton sat up and said, "Has it been such a long time that you've forgotten me, my friend? I am Taro, whom you killed and robbed. I have been waiting here, hoping that I would meet you again some day."

Terrified, Jiro turned to run, but the skeleton seized his *kimono* in its bony hand, and would not let him escape.

"Don't be so quick to run away. Tell me what you have been doing since you struck me down."

Choking with fear, Jiro told how he had gone home and spent all Taro's money and was now going to the city to become a thief.

"You haven't changed," said the skeleton. "But you are sure to come to a bad end if you become a thief. I have a better idea. I will dance like this—" Here the skeleton began to dance, rattling and clattering his bones together, waving his arms in the air and kicking with his legs. Then he continued, "You can put me in a box and carry me around with you, and people will pay you to see me dance. Since I won't eat or wear clothes, and money means nothing to me, you can earn a great deal without expense."

"Why should you do this for me?" asked Jiro, though his mind was already filled with pictures of the fortune he could earn.

"I am bound to you in death as in life," said Taro. "Will you accept my offer?"

"Yes," said Jiro. Then he took the skeleton and pur-

chased a beautiful teakwood chest to store it in, and toured the countryside, playing a flute while the skeleton danced in front of wondering crowds. The money poured in, enough so that Jiro could spend it as fast and foolishly as before, and still have some left over.

Eventually word of Jiro and his dancing skeleton reached the most powerful lord of the province. He summoned Jiro to his castle and told him to have the skeleton dance in the vast hall that was filled with his guests.

Jiro opened the chest, stretched Taro's skeleton out on the bamboo matting, and began to play a lively tune on his flute. But the skeleton simply lay there. Jiro played tune after tune, then began to yell and curse, but the skeleton refused to move.

Finally, in a rage, Jiro took his flute and began to beat upon the bones, commanding them to get up and dance.

At that moment, the skeleton sat up, climbed to its feet, and walked to the throne of the great lord. There, bowing humbly, it said, "My lord, I have been dancing all this time, just so word would reach you, and I would be brought before you. In my life, I was your honest subject, Taro. This fellow killed me and robbed me of my money." Then the skeleton told exactly how this had happened.

The lord, who was a just man, was angered at the way Jiro had betrayed his friend. "Seize that man, and take him away to be tried!" he ordered his guards.

At that moment the skeleton fell to pieces before the throne; and three days later Jiro was sentenced to death for his crimes.

Scared to Death

(United States—South Carolina)

Some ten years after the Civil War, the old Charleston mansion named Roseway was ablaze with lights and bursting with music. An orchestra, hired by Stephen Heyward, played waltz after waltz in the huge ballroom in honor of his daughter Sally's eighteenth birthday.

Sally, however, had quickly grown bored with the whole affair and had steered a cluster of handsome young men and beautiful young women to the open area at the foot of the magnificent staircase. There she stood, rearranging her pale yellow skirts that rose, ruffle upon ruffle, to her waist. Her bare shoulders were adorned with a single fall of jet-black hair, which tumbled over her left shoulder. A perfect red rose was pinned to her bodice, setting off the whiteness of her skin.

Even if she hadn't been mistress of Roseway since her mother's untimely death—or hadn't flirted so outrageously—Sally would have easily drawn the attention of the young men now gathered around her because of her beauty. Her dark eyes, ivory skin, and bubbling laughter charmed men of all ages.

At the moment, however, she was quiet. She was looking

unabashedly at tall, dark Peter Beaufort, while listening intently to what Alice Cardross, his fiancée, was saying.

Breathlessly Alice informed the little cluster of friends, "When our carriage passed the graveyard tonight, both horses reared up. I declare, I was so frightened, I almost lost my wits."

"I'm sure nothing serious was at risk," said Sally, with a wicked little smile.

Gallantly Peter said, "It's certainly spooky there—I've heard the place is haunted."

"Yes," said Sally, sounding even more bored than before, "we've all *heard* stories, but have you ever *seen* a ghost, Peter?"

"Don't *you* believe in ghosts?" asked Alice, in a voice barely above a whisper.

"Not at all," sneered Sally. "Only simpletons hold with such foolishness."

"My manservant saw a ghost standing by old Daniel Payson's tombstone," said Peter. "That's the tallest grave marker—the one that tilts to one side. The ghost was the image of Daniel Payson, who's been dead four years."

"Bosh!" said Sally, with an airy wave of her hand. "Your man dreamed it—or was frightened by a shadow."

"You'd never catch *me* going into the cemetery after dark," said Alice, holding more tightly to Peter's arm.

"Why? Whatever on earth is there to be afraid of, *really?*" wondered Sally, ignoring Alice to stare into Peter's face.

Peter, who seemed equally uncomfortable with Alice's clinging and Sally's boasting, said, "Come, now, Sally, you wouldn't go in there after dark, and you know it!"

"Nonsense!" Sally retorted angrily. "I'm not as foolish as some people I know." She looked pointedly at Alice.

Alice, aware that Sally was making fun of her, cried, "If

you're so brave, I dare you to go into the graveyard alone. Tonight. *Right now!*"

"Oh, very well," said Sally offhandedly. "Peter, will you escort me?" She stretched out her hand to take his.

But the young man put his arm around Alice's shoulder and said, "I've never been a man to tempt fate, Miss Heyward."

Nor would any of the other young gentlemen surrounding her risk the unknown terrors of the churchyard—even for a chance to escort the lovely Sally.

"Then I'll go alone," snapped Sally pettishly. "The dead couldn't be any more dreary company than the rest of you!" She sent one of her servants to the cloakroom to fetch her wrap.

"Wait," said Alice. She ran after the servant and returned with Peter's walking cane, which had a gold handle shaped like a goblin's head. While Sally was putting on her wrap, Alice thrust the cane at her, saying, "Take this, and plant it in the ground by old man Payson's crooked tombstone. That way, we'll know in the morning that you really went there."

"Since my word isn't good enough for you, Miss Cardross," Sally said nastily, "you'll find the cane in the morning—when the sunlight gives you enough courage to look for it!" Then, gathering her long cloak around her, Sally Heyward swept out through the front door and into the night.

She marched along the moonlit sidewalk to the cemetery, slashing at the air in front of her with the gold-tipped cane, furious at the memory of how Peter Beaufort had defended his fiancée, Alice Cardross, against Sally's best efforts to belittle the other woman. And she grew even angrier at the thought that he remained unmoved by Sally's charms—in spite of the fact that she had flirted with him throughout the whole evening.

Sally pushed open the high iron gates in the churchyard wall and stepped through. Inside was complete darkness, except for an occasional tall grave marker gleaming palely in the moonlight. Dimly the young woman could see the outline of the church steeple on the far side of the cemetery. Though she couldn't make out the face of the clock in the tower, she clearly heard it chiming midnight.

Up until this moment, Sally had been angry and not in the least afraid. But the thick, chill darkness pressed closely in on her, creating shadows that seemed to writhe and clutch at her when she didn't look directly at them. Deciding, with a last burst of resentment, that this was the wretched end to an already spoiled evening, she wrapped her cloak more tightly about her, and searched hastily for the crooked tombstone.

A part of her was ready to cut and run, but Sally was strong-willed enough to force herself to make good her boast. She would plant the cane before she left or die in the attempt. Keeping this thought in mind, she searched up and down the narrow rows of tombstones, until she discovered the crooked marker, shining faintly in the moonlight.

She raised the cane to thrust it into the damp soil below the marble slab, then froze—

A sigh, then a loud moan, came from the blackness just beyond the tombstone. A sudden gust of wind, chill and smelling of damp and mold, rushed past her. She was certain that she could hear something coming toward her —something that moved stiffly and wetly and never drew a mortal breath.

Stifling a scream, Sally thrust Peter's cane into the ground; then, gathering up her cloak, she turned to run.

Something caught her; something held her and wouldn't

let her run. She heard a moan and smelled the breath of the open grave. But the more frantically she struggled, the more firmly the horror held her in its grip. Too frightened to scream, she clawed frantically toward the narrow aisle of tombstones that led back to the gate. But something was tugging at her throat now. In a final spasm of terror, she flung herself forward, only to feel herself dragged back toward the crooked tombstone. At that moment something burst in her head, and she sank to the ground, mercifully unconscious.

When Sally failed to return, Peter and Alice led a party of anxious friends and relatives into the churchyard.

There they found Sally, a short distance from the crooked tombstone, dead, her eyes wide open in fear. The end of her cloak was pinned solidly to the ground at the foot of the marble slab—held in place by the deeply planted cane with the gold goblin's head. The unfortunate young woman had scared herself to death.

To this day, people talk of *two* ghosts that haunt the old churchyard. One is the tall shadowy figure of a man; the other is a woman in a pale yellow dress with a long cloak, who wears a single red rose in her bodice.

Swallowed Alive

(a British folktale)

Dorothy Mately lived in the British town of Ashover in the county of Derby during the seventeenth century. She was a widow who made a living working for a lead mine located nearby. She would take the ore which had been dug out of the mine, break it with a hammer, and wash this to separate out the traces of lead from the other minerals.

She was a big, homely, rough-spoken woman who upset many of her neighbors with her continual cursing and swearing. She was also rumored to be a liar and thief, but she would deny this loudly if anybody accused her. Her favorite expression was "Let God open the earth and have it swallow me, if what I tell you isn't the truth."

On the morning, of March 23, 1660, while she was busy washing ore in a stream near the mine, a young miner, just off his shift, decided to take a quick plunge in the water to clean off the day's grime from working below. He slipped off his trousers and laid them on a rock while he swam in the brisk mountain stream.

When he climbed out a short time later, he discovered his clothing had been tossed about, and his pockets had been searched. Several coins, which had been in the young man's pocket, were missing. Since they were all he had to live on until the next payday, he frantically searched for the thief. But the only one he spotted was Dorothy, hard at work with her tub and sieve, seemingly unaware of the hue and cry the lad was raising.

Because there was not a sign of anyone else around, he accused her of stealing his money and demanded she give it back.

Holding her ore hammer tightly in one hand, Dorothy stood up and loudly denied she knew anything about the missing coins. As usual, she ended this by saying, "Let God open the earth and have it swallow me, if what I'm telling you isn't the truth."

As it happened, a God-fearing man from Ashover was passing nearby and overheard the argument. He knew Dorothy's reputation, and he knew that her accuser was an honest, hard-working young man, who would never call someone a thief without good reason. He took a step forward in the hope of helping to resolve the argument when Dorothy suddenly cursed the miner and threatened him with her hammer.

Startled, the young man turned and ran.

The passerby walked over to Dorothy and said he had witnessed the whole event. He demanded that the woman restore the money she had stolen.

Because the newcomer was a man of some importance in the village, Dorothy did not threaten him. She merely insisted on her innocence and made up some story about having seen two men lurking near the stream shortly before the theft was discovered. The man did not believe a word of this and told her so, threatening to involve the authorities in the matter.

At this, Dorothy raised her hammer in her right hand over her head and cried, "Let God open the earth and have it swallow me, if what I've told you isn't the truth!"

Disgusted, the fellow turned to continue on his way. But he had gone only a few paces, when he heard Dorothy scream. Looking back, he was dumbfounded to see her spinning round and round like a top, all the while sinking into the ground with her tub and sieve, her hammer still raised over her head.

Even while he stared, the woman disappeared into what seemed to be a whirlpool in the solid earth. Suddenly it stopped, and the man cautiously crept to the edge of the opening. Below him, he saw Dorothy some nine feet down; the woman was buried almost to her waist in the loose earth, which had completely covered her working tools.

The villager frantically tried to think of a way to help her. Lowering his coat toward her, he said, "Take hold of this, and pray God will pardon your sin and let you live."

"I have no sin to forgive," she said, stretching her fingers toward his dangling coat sleeve. But immediately she began spinning and sinking again. In a moment she was far below her rescuer's reach. She screeched for help, now buried almost to her shoulders in the soil.

"I hope God will have mercy on you," the man called down, "for I'm afraid you will never be seen alive again."

But Dorothy only struggled harder to raise herself out of the soft earth. Suddenly a large stone apparently tumbled from nowhere, and struck her soundly on the head, silencing her screams and curses. As if this was a signal, loose earth from the mouth of the opening began pouring down on her and quickly buried the wretched woman, while the man scrambled back from the crumbling edge.

When workmen from the mine eventually dug Dorothy Mately's lifeless body from the pit, they found she had sunk some twelve feet down. There was no sign of her hammer, tub, or sieve.

When her body was laid out on the grass, the miners found the young man's stolen coins in her apron pocket.

The Deacon's Ghost

(a folktale from Iceland)

Many years ago, in Iceland, a deacon served in the parish of a small town, nestled in the side of a beautiful little valley. He was very much in love with a girl named Gudrun, who lived in a farm on the opposite side of the valley, across the river from his own tidy little house near his church. They were engaged to be married in the spring.

He had a handsome horse with a gray mane. He called the horse Shadow and rode him every day.

A short time before Christmas, the young man rode to Gudrun's home and invited her to join in the Christmas Eve celebration at the church. He promised to come for her on Shadow, so they could ride back together. She was delighted and said she would watch for him in the evening, so they could leave without delay. Then she brought him tea and cakes, and they passed a long afternoon planning for their future life together.

Earlier in the day he had ridden safely across the frozen river because the ice was so thick. But even while the deacon and his betrothed were talking, an unseasonable thaw had set in. The river became a flood; much of the ice broke up and was whirled downstream in huge drifts.

When the young man left the farm late in the day, he was so full of happy dreams that he did not immediately notice how much the river had changed. As soon as it became clear to him what the situation was, he searched rapidly for a means of crossing the treacherous stream. Spotting a bridge of ice that still spanned the river, he urged Shadow onto this. But when they reached the middle, the bridge crumbled beneath them and tumbled the horse and rider into the stream.

The next morning a search party was sent out when it was found that the deacon had not returned home. Later in the day Shadow was discovered running free across a frosty meadow. Shortly after that, the searchers found the corpse of the deacon, which had drifted to the bank after the man had drowned. All the flesh had been torn off the back of his head, so the skull shone through.

Sadly they brought the body back to the town, and the deacon was buried a week before Christmas.

As it happened, the river continued to flood so dangerously that no one from one side of the valley could cross to the other. No one had been able to bring word to Gudrun of the deacon's death. Having no idea of the tragedy that had befallen, she happily looked forward to Christmas Eve when her lover would come for her and take her across the river to the celebration at his church.

On Christmas Eve, while she was still dressing in her finest clothes, Gudrun heard a knock at the door. A moment later one of the maids opened the door but saw no one there. Since the moon was quite hidden by clouds, the girl went to fetch a light. But holding a lamp high over her head, she could discover no one. Puzzled, she returned to her work.

A short time later the knock was repeated. Gudrun, who

was just pulling on her winter cloak, called, "It is someone waiting for me."

She pulled open the door and saw Shadow standing a short distance away. The figure of the deacon, his hat pulled low over his eyes, stood beside the horse. She hurried to him, and without a word he helped her climb onto Shadow. Then he mounted in front of her, and they rode off in the direction of the river. As they rode, the moon slid out from behind the clouds, so it was very easy to see again.

When they reached the stream, Gudrun saw that it was frozen over again, except for a narrow ribbon of black water in the middle, where the current kept the frost from hardening.

Quickly the horse trotted onto the ice, then leaped over the rapid stream in the middle. At the moment they lighted on the far side, the deacon's head bobbed forward so that his hat slipped over his eyes for a moment. Gudrun saw a large patch of bare skull gleaming white in the middle of his hair.

"What has happened to your head, my love?" the girl asked.

"Ride a little farther with me, and you'll understand" was all her lover would say as he set his hat back in place.

Troubled, Gudrun looked eagerly toward the lights of town, gleaming across the frosty fields and drifting snow.

But instead of going to the church, which was ablaze with lights, the deacon turned Shadow toward the churchyard beside it. He brought them to a halt outside the ice-crusted hedges. Without a word, he dismounted and helped Gudrun down.

Shivering, the girl asked, "Why have we stopped here, my love?"

He put out his hand, which felt as cold as the ice all

around, to lead her through the hedge gate, saying, "Walk a little farther with me, and you'll understand."

The young woman let him lead her amid the snow-dusted tombstones, wondering what strange notion had taken possession of him. But when they had reached the center of the cemetery, she saw that they were heading for an open grave, which had frozen earth piled up all around it.

"My love, why are you showing me this?" she asked in a voice made small by her fear.

"Just rest beside me there, and you'll understand," the deacon said.

Sick with horror, Gudrun broke free and began to run to the church porch, screaming for help. Suddenly she felt her cloak snatched from behind. For a desperate moment she was held prisoner; then she loosened the clasp and ran on toward the church, where shouts and bobbing lights showed people were coming to help her.

Just as she stumbled into the arms of her rescuers, she looked behind her. She saw the deacon jump headlong into the open grave, with her cloak hugged to him. The piles of dirt on either side tumbled in after him, filling the grave once again.

But the troubled ghost of the deacon came night after night to try and drag Gudrun away with him, so that she had to be guarded from sunrise to sunset. The priest from a neighboring parish tried to lay the spirit to rest; but nothing worked until a man from the north, who knew something about ancient spells, came and drove out the demon who possessed the man's body. After that, the deacon remained at rest, never to haunt Gudrun again.

Nuckelavee

(a folktale from the Orkney Islands)

The people of the Orkney Islands, off the north-eastern coast of Scotland, tell many stories of a monster called Nuckelavee, who lived in the sea but never missed a chance to plague humankind whenever he could. When he came onshore, he appeared as a horse and rider—though, in fact, a closer look showed man and horse were all part of the same creature.

His human-looking head was ten times the size of a normal man's, while the horselike head had an enormous mouth that jutted out like a pig's. Most horrible of all, he seemed to have no skin, so those who came near and lived to tell of it, swore that you could see black blood flowing through his veins, and every movement of his white muscles.

If crops withered away, or livestock fell off the high rocks that made up the shoreline, or a disease plagued the islanders, the folk blamed Nuckelavee. They said his breath was poisonous, bringing blight and disease wherever he trod.

The only thing the monster feared was fresh water, and he would never cross a running stream. Nor would he ever visit the land when it was raining.

There was once an old man named Thomas, who met the monster late one night. Though there was no moon, the air was clear and the stars gave considerable light. Thomas was going home from an evening in the village, and his path lay close by the seashore.

Just as he began the most dangerous part of his journey, where the road ran along a ridge, with the sea on one side and a deep, freshwater lake on the other, he saw a huge shape ahead, moving toward him.

He sensed instantly that it was no natural thing he was facing. He could not move to either side, because of the water that hemmed in the path; and he had heard that turning one's back on an evil thing was the worst thing a man could do.

"The Lord be with me and take care of me," Thomas whispered to himself. Then, since he was always regarded as brave or foolhardy (depending on the person one talked with), he decided, as the best of two evils, to face whatever was coming toward him. So he walked slowly but steadily forward.

He quickly discovered to his horror that the gruesome creature approaching him was the dreaded Nuckelavee. Thomas could see quite clearly that the lower part of this terrible monster was indeed like a horse, with flippers extending from his legs. The mouth seemed large as a whale's mouth, gleaming with sharp teeth in the starlight and giving off breath that poured out like steam from a giant teakettle. The horsehead had a single eye, glowing red as a coal.

Out of the back grew what seemed to be the upper half of a man, with a head as big as a barrel and arms that reached nearly to the ground. The whole creature looked sculpted from red, raw flesh, in which Thomas saw blood black as tar, running in yellow veins, and great white sinews twisting, stretching, and contracting as the monster moved.

In mortal terror—his hair standing on end and his body feeling as if it was filmed with ice—Thomas forced himself to keep moving. He knew it would be useless to try to escape and determined to die facing his enemy, rather than with his back to the monster.

Then, for all his fear, the man remembered what he had heard of Nuckelavee's dislike of fresh water. So he edged closer to the side of the road near the lake.

The awful moment came when the lower head of the monster was just inches from him. To the terrified man, the mouth of the creature yawned like a bottomless pit. The red eye seemed to burn into his mind. Slowly the long arms were stretched out to seize Thomas.

At the last possible instant, the man ducked under one arm and ran forward, splashing through the shallows of the lake. Some of the water sprinkled the foreleg of the monster. The horsehead snorted like thunder, and the monster shied over to the far side of the road.

Without looking around, Thomas began running with all his might; behind him he heard Nuckelavee turn and gallop after him; the mannish head bellowed with a sound like a typhoon ripping across the sea.

Ahead of Thomas was a little stream, by which water from the lake overflowed into the sea. The man knew if he could only cross the running water, he was safe; so he strained every muscle to reach safety.

Behind him he felt the wind of Nuckelavee's clutches as he narrowly escaped the monster's grip. Just as he reached the bank of the little stream, the long arms snatched at him again. Thomas made a desperate leap, felt his cap and part of his coat torn away by Nuckelavee, then landed safely on the far side, just out of reach of the monster.

Nuckelavee gave a deafening, unearthly yell of disappointment and rage, as his victim raced to safety beyond the water.

Thomas continued to run until he knew for certain that he was safe. When he finally stopped to glance back toward the grotesque Nuckelavee, he could still hear the creature's terrifying roar, but the sight of the monster would be only a memory from now on.

The Adventure of the German Student

(from a tale by Washington Irving)

Gottfried Wolfgang was a young man of a good family. He had gone to school for a time in his native Germany, but he had become so obsessed with studies about spirits and devils and who knows what that it began to affect his mind and health. He was especially tormented by the idea that a demon was haunting him, trying to catch him and ensure his ruin.

He became thin and gloomy. His friends, determined to help him, decided that the best cure was a change of scene. So they sent him to finish studies amid the splendors and gayeties of Paris.

Unhappily Wolfgang arrived just as the French Revolution was breaking out. The terrible scenes of violence that followed shocked his sensitive nature, disgusted him with society and the world, and made him even more solitary in his ways. He kept to himself in a lonely apartment in the old part of Paris where most students who attended the university lived.

In his loneliness, he would often daydream of the face of a beautiful woman. Her imagined features made so strong an impression on him that he dreamed of her again and again. She began to haunt his thoughts by day and his sleep at night. He fell passionately in love with this shadow of a dream.

One stormy night young Wolfgang was returning to his lodgings. The hour was late, and a storm had just begun. Loud thunderclaps rolled through the dark narrow streets, filled with driving rain. Lightning danced over the peaked roofs above him and shed flickering gleams over the open space in front of him. This was the square where public executions were performed—a place he dreaded to cross even in the sunlight.

The rain came down harder, driven by a freezing wind. Wolfgang rushed out into the square, but stumbled and fell to his knees. As he picked himself up, he was horrified to find himself close by the guillotine—the dreadful instrument of death that stood ever ready to claim fresh victims.

Shuddering, the young man was turning from the horrible engine when he saw a shadowy form cowering at the foot of the steps that led up to the scaffold. Several vivid flashes of lightning revealed the figure more distinctly: it was a woman dressed in black. She was seated on one of the lower steps of the platform, leaning forward, her face hidden in her hands. Her long, tangled hair was streaming with the rain that fell in torrents.

Wolfgang paused. There was something touching and terrible in this solitary figure of woe. He guessed she was some heartbroken mourner whose relative or lover had been cut away from her by the dreadful blade. His heart went out to her suffering.

He approached her and said gently, "Mademoiselle, you will catch your death out here."

She raised her head and looked wildly at him. He was astonished to see, in the bright glare of the lightning, the very face which had haunted him in his dreams. Her fea-

tures were pale and grief-stricken, but she was ravishingly beautiful.

Trembling with unexpected emotion, Wolfgang urged her, "You should not be out here at this hour, exposed to the fury of such a storm. I beg you, permit me to take you to some friends."

In answer, she merely pointed to the guillotine, and shook her head. "I have no friend on earth," she said sadly.

"But you must have a home," said Wolfgang.

"Yes—in the grave!"

The heart of the student melted at these words.

"If a stranger can make an offer, without danger of being misunderstood," said he, "I would offer my humble rooms as shelter, and make myself your devoted friend. I am friendless myself in Paris, and a stranger in the land—but whatever help I can give you, it is yours for the asking."

There was such an honest earnestness in the young man's manner that the homeless stranger nodded her head, as if too wearied by her suffering to do more.

Sharing his cloak with her, he led her from the square and the sight of the horrible instrument of execution.

On entering his apartment, the student, for the first time, felt how shabby his rooms were. They were cluttered with books and papers and all the other things a student uses. Hastily he cleared off a chair by the fireplace. Then he lit candles and a small fire to let his visitor warm herself, for her hands were cold as ice.

In the firelight, he had a better opportunity of studying her; and he found himself even more intoxicated by her beauty. Her pale face had a dazzling fairness that was set off by the clusters of raven hair framing it. Her eyes were large and brilliant, though something like wildness swam in their depths. Her whole appearance was striking, but she was dressed in a simple black dress with only one item of jewelery: a broad black band around her neck, clasped with a diamond pin.

"I will spend the night with another student, whose apartment is above," Wolfgang offered. But he was so fascinated by the woman's charms, there seemed to be such a spell upon his thoughts and senses that he could not tear himself from her presence. Instead they sat and talked, while the rain continued to beat against the windowpanes, and thunder rattled the shutters.

She spoke but little and never mentioned the guillotine. Her grief abated, but she would not say what had caused it. For the most part she contented herself, listening to him and staring into the fire.

Wolfgang, in the infatuation of the moment, confessed his love for her. He told her the story of his mysterious dream and how she had possessed his heart before he had even seen her.

She seemed strangely affected by his recital and admitted, "From the first, I was drawn to you by a power I cannot account for either."

The young man saw that his kindness, which had first won her confidence, had now apparently won her heart. It was a time for wild actions, and Wolfgang suddenly knelt beside her chair, saying, "You have no home or family. Let me be everything to you—or, rather, let us be everything to one another. Marry me—here is my hand," and he grabbed her delicate hand in his own, distressed to feel how cold it still was. "I pledge myself to you forever!" he said, in the heat of his own passion, "upon my very soul."

"Forever? Upon your soul?" said the stranger solemnly.

"Forever!" repeated Wolfgang. "My heart and soul are yours."

The stranger clasped his fingers tightly in her own.

"Then I am yours," she murmured and kissed him. "And you are mine . . . forever." Then she whispered, "Now, help me to the bed, for I am growing so tired, so very tired."

Alarmed at the weakness in her voice, Wolfgang escorted her to the little bed in the next room. She fell asleep the instant her head touched the pillow. Quietly he withdrew and spent the few hours left of the night dreaming of the life he and the stranger would build for themselves.

The next morning, while she was still sleeping, the student went out to look for a more spacious apartment suitable for his bride. The storm had passed, and the streets gleamed with sunlight, reflecting brightly off lingering puddles. He quickly found new lodgings, arranged to take possession of them immediately, and returned to his rooms.

But when he threw open the bedroom door and called to the woman, he found her lying with her head hanging over the bed, with one arm thrown over it. He spoke to her and received no reply. He advanced to awaken her from her uncomfortable position. Lifting her hand, he discovered it was cold, without a trace of pulse. Her fair face was now pallid and ghastly. He knew in an instant that she was a corpse.

Horrified and frantic, he awoke the house. In the confusion that followed, someone had sense enough to summon the police. As the officer entered the room, he started back the moment he saw the body.

"Great heaven!" he cried. "How did this woman come here?"

"Do you know anything about her?" asked Wolfgang through his tears.

"Of course!" exclaimed the officer. "She was guillotined yesterday."

He stepped forward, undid the black collar around the neck of the corpse, and the head rolled on the floor!

The student began to shriek, "The demon! The demon has gained possession of me! I am lost forever."

Vainly they tried to calm him. But he was possessed by the frightful belief that an evil spirit had brought the dead body back to life and tricked him into pledging away his soul forever.

With a cry he ran out into the street and was never seen in Paris again. Years later the rumor circulated that he had returned to his native Germany, where he died in a madhouse, still believing himself possessed by a demon.

Billy Mosby's Night Ride

(United States—New England)

In the early 1800s, in a small town in a remote part of New York state, a young boy named Billy Mosby, whose parents had died, was raised by his grandparents, Enoch and Anne Mosby.

Billy helped out on his grandparents' farm, getting up early to milk the cows and feed the pigs and gather the eggs. Though he sometimes grumbled when his grandfather rousted him out of bed before sunrise, he liked his new life and found little to complain about.

He was afraid, however, of his grandparents' neighbor, Francis Woolcott, who lived a half mile down the road from them. Every afternoon, when the sun was westering and long shadows had begun to creep down the hillsides, Billy would watch from a window as Francis Woolcott, like a tall, dark shadow, strode down the dusty road toward the grove of ash and chestnut trees at the end of the road.

He lived in a cabin, which he had let fall nearly to ruin. But he never wanted for anything. The farmers whispered that he was a witch—and feared him so much that they gave him pork, flour, meal, cider, or anything that he might need. If they didn't, neighbors said, he would make a horse come to a dead halt in the middle of plowing, or make a man run around, flapping his folded arms like wings and clucking like a chicken. But even worse, rumor said, was the fact that the old man could conjure up thirteen night riders—demons straight from hell—when the moon was growing old. They would go anywhere he told them to, and do all sorts of mischief. Whenever he heard about the demon riders, Billy felt a thrill of fear—and an eagerness to see these creatures of the night (from a safe distance, of course).

Woolcott never bothered Billy's grandparents. They were polite to the man when they met him in the lane, and thought the talk of witchery was so much foolishness. "Good Christian folk should be about their business and not wasting time scaring each other with such nonsense," declared Anne Mosby.

But Billy kept an open mind; there was so much talk in the neighborhood, he couldn't believe *everybody* was wrong. He kept his thoughts to himself, however: he knew there was no arguing with his grandparents once their minds were made up.

But Billy's curiosity about Francis Woolcott grew the more he tried not to think about the strange old man.

"I've got to see for myself," he decided one evening. So after his grandparents were asleep in their room, he slipped out his bedroom window and ran down the road to Woolcott's cabin. A three-quarter moon overhead gave plenty of light to see by.

But when he was near the dark cabin, Billy saw the old man open the front door. The boy ducked behind a bush; but, peeking from behind some leaves, he saw that Woolcott was carrying bundles of oat straw in his arms. With a quick glance up and down the road, the shadowy figure headed toward the grove of ash and chestnut trees at the end of the lane.

When it seemed safe, Billy followed. Something told him that tonight he would find out the truth about Woolcott's witchery.

The man went directly to a clearing in the center of the grove. There he carefully laid out thirteen bundles of oat straw in a circle. Standing inside this ring, Woolcott extended his arms and began to turn, muttering words that Billy, watching around the trunk of a chestnut tree, could not hear.

As the witch spun faster, the bundles of oat straw began to put off sprouts so they looked as if they were growing into gnarly plants. But the "roots" quickly became horses' legs, the bundles themselves became the bodies of sleek black horses, and the strange "blossoms" became their heads and tails.

Then a cloud passed across the moon, and the clearing was suddenly dark. When the moonlight returned, Billy saw that there was now a rider on the back of each horse. They were wrapped in black cloaks and had their broad-brimmed hats drawn down so that the boy could see nothing of their faces.

Quickly Francis Woolcott began giving instructions to these mysterious horsemen, sending them off in different directions. Sometimes a night rider would go alone; sometimes two would gallop off together. When all but one had been sent away, Billy, leaning closer to try and hear what Woolcott was saying, stepped on a dry, fallen branch that gave a loud *SNAP!*

Instantly the man at the center of the clearing came bounding across and grabbed the boy before he could run. Woolcott's hand was like a claw on Billy's shoulder as he hauled the boy into the clearing, where the last night rider silently waited.

"Please don't hurt me!" begged Billy. "I promise I won't tell."

"Tell whomever you please," said the man. "It doesn't matter a jot to me." Then he fixed Billy with a thoughtful stare and stroked his chin. "It might just be I could use a brave lad like you as an apprentice. You've got curiosity enough to kill a cat nine times over. And you seem bright enough." Now Woolcott was rubbing his hands together eagerly. "Yes, you have all the makings of a fine apprentice. So we'll begin your lessons tonight: since you were curious about my friend, ride with him awhile—satisfy your curiosity."

Before Billy could even ask what an "apprentice" was, the old man picked him up with surprising strength and swung him onto the saddle, behind the shadowy rider. "Now go!" the old man yelled.

Without a word, the rider urged his midnight steed to a trot and guided the animal out of the clearing to the road. Billy found he was stuck to the sleek, black horse as though he were a part of it. He glanced once over his shoulder and saw Francis Woolcott standing in the clearing, watching him. The rider in front said nothing; but Billy felt him urging his horse to a gallop, the moment they were free of the trees.

In uncanny silence they rushed down the lane. The silky black cloak of the man in front of him whipped back around Billy, obscuring his view much of the time. The horses' hoofs made no sound on the rock-strewn roadway; the only sound was the wind rushing past the boy's ears. They raced like hurricanes across fields and through woods—leaping bushes, fences, even *trees* without effort.

Billy lost all track of time and distance. He began to think they were going to ride forever, when they reached the gates of a farm Billy had never seen before. The house was quiet and dark.

Reining in his horse in front of the barn, the night rider cried:

> "Tangle the horses' tails this night;
> Let the hogs all sing and dance upright."

The doors of the barn flew open, and two horses charged into the yard. They whinnied in terror, and Billy could see their tails were so twisted together that they began running in a circle, which only frightened them more. Behind them, in the shadows of the barn, he saw the nightmarish forms of three pigs, squealing and prancing around on their hind legs, as though they were trying to sing and dance.

Lamps were lit in the farmhouse; Billy could hear shouts. The night rider wheeled his horse and galloped away from the farm. They traveled fast as a whirlwind through unfamiliar countryside. Long after the moon had set, Billy began to recognize landmarks. In the starlight he saw that they were nearing the cluster of chestnut and ash trees where his adventure had begun.

But at the very edge of the grove, Billy's rider suddenly vanished; the black horse turned into a bundle of oat straw under him, and he tumbled to the ground with a *thump*.

He lay for a long time, just catching his breath. Then he got to his feet, grabbed the bundle of oat straw, and ran to tell his grandparents what he had seen. Before he reached home, he looked at the oat straw and thought, "They'll never believe me." So he crept quietly back into bed and said nothing, though in his mind he relived the amazing night ride again and again.

The next evening, sitting at the kitchen table helping his grandmother shell peas, Billy asked, "What's an 'apprentice'?"

"A beginner, a learner," Anne Mosby answered, "a boy who works for someone so he can learn the man's trade." She looked at her grandson curiously. "You thinking of hiring yourself out to someone?"

"No," said Billy, "I just heard the word somewhere, and I wondered what it meant."

But as he worked at the peas, his mind began to race. He imagined what it might be like to wave his hands and have pigs dance in the moonlight or bundles of oat straw turn into night riders on magical horses. If he could ever get up the nerve, he thought, he might, just *might,* ask Francis Woolcott to make him an apprentice. It was a frightening thought, but it was also an exciting one.

But there were no more stories of the thirteen night riders after that. Though Billy eagerly watched the road past the farm, old Francis Woolcott, who was ninety years old, no longer visited the neighbors and took away the farmers' goods with him. The boy heard several people mutter, "He's died or gone to the devil, and not a moment too soon."

No one would go near the silent, tumble-down cabin. When Billy suggested he and his grandparents should go take a look, Anne and Enoch told him to mind his own business.

When his need to know what had happened and his fear that he might never learn the secrets of night riding got the better of him, Billy slipped away one afternoon to the little house that looked completely deserted. He knocked several times; when a faint cry came from inside, the boy pushed open the door.

The cramped room inside smelled stale and sour. Old Francis Woolcott lay under a pile of filthy bedclothes on a cot in one corner. At first Billy thought the old man was dead, his eyes were closed so tight. But they popped open, and Woolcott asked sharply, "What are you doing here, boy?"

"I . . . well . . . ," Billy mumbled.

"Speak up!" Francis Woolcott demanded.

"I want to become your apprentice," the boy managed to get out.

"Then you're a fool, boy," said the old man bitterly. "Why would you want to learn such things?"

"I want to call up night riders of my own," Billy said eagerly. "I want to be able to turn people I don't like into chickens."

"There's a price on such secrets, boy," whispered the old man, suddenly turning his head to watch the door. "There's a terrible price which nobody should have to pay. But I'm going to, soon enough."

"What do you mean?" asked Billy, wondering if maybe the old man had gone out of his head.

"*He's* coming for me soon," croaked Francis Woolcott. "I'm dying, but I won't have any peace."

"Maybe I'd better go get my grandfather," said Billy, frightened by the other's fear. He turned to go, but the old man grabbed his wrist with a clutch like a circle of iron.

Billy heard a sudden clap of thunder, unexpected on what had been a pleasant summer day. Staring out the window, he saw rain pelting down from a sudden storm. In the shadows, the dying man's face had such a horrible look that Billy gave a small cry of alarm. With each peal of thunder, Woolcott trembled more and more.

"*He's* coming," the old man said again, struggling to sit up in bed. Then he gave a cry and fell back on his pillow.

Billy heard the loudest crash of thunder yet. Then, over the sound of the wind and rain, he heard galloping hoofs in the road. They stopped just outside the cabin.

Francis Woolcott, terror-stricken, tightened his hold on the boy, and tried to say something that Billy couldn't make out. The door was flung open, and a night rider stood like a monstrous shadow in the doorway. The old man gave a final, strangulated cry, then let his hand drop limply away from Billy's wrist.

There was a violet flash of lightning; for an instant Billy caught a glimpse of the rider's face. He saw horns, skin the color of raw beef, and eyes that burned like coals. The room smelled of sulfur, and the sound of rain on the roof was deafening. Then the figure strode to the bed, picked up the old man as if he weighed no more than a bundle of oat straw, and carried him through the door.

The panel slammed behind them. There was a peal of thunder, then the sound of galloping hoofs disappearing into the rain.

But when Billy had calmed down enough to leave the cabin that now held only him, he found the road outside was dry. At home he found his grandparents hadn't noticed any rain or heard any thunder. When he tried to tell them what he had seen, they scolded him for making up outlandish stories.

Later Anne asked her grandson, "You still thinking about becoming someone's apprentice?"

"No, ma'am," said Billy, "not now, not *ever!*"

The Hunter in the Haunted Forest

(a Native American legend)

Once a young hunter of the Teton tribe went seeking game in a forest that was supposed to be haunted. His relatives and friends tried to discourage him from going there. But he said, "I have a wife and two children to feed. Winter is coming, and luck has been against me. We have very little to eat. If I don't bring back game, my family will starve."

"We will share what we have with you," promised his relatives.

"No," he said, "if the winter lingers, and my family eats too much of your food, we will all starve. I have heard there is much game in those woods because no one goes there."

"That is because ghosts roam its paths at night," said his friends. "Anyone who goes there does not come back."

But the young man's mind was made up. He took a small quantity of *wasna*, which is grease mixed with pounded buffalo meat and wild cherry. His father gave him some tobacco to take with him, also.

Then he set out. After two days he reached the edge of the haunted forest. Just as he entered its shadows, the Thunder Beings raised a great storm, so he was forced to seek shelter from the pounding rain. Hurrying along the path, he came to a clearing. In the center was a small tepee made of deer hide.

Just as the hunter was about to lift the flap and go inside, he heard two persons talking.

One voice said, "Hush! There is someone outside. Let us invite him in. We will offer him food and invite him to stay the night here. Then, when he is asleep, we will kill him and follow his ghost along the spirit's road"—which is what the Teton people called the Milky Way.

"Yes, yes," the other voice agreed eagerly.

Then the hunter fled, because he knew they were ghosts inside the tepee. And he knew from their talk that they had not found their way out of this world, but walked a dark trail—probably because they had been wicked when they were alive.

So he ran until he thought his lungs and heart would burst. For a time he was sure he heard the ghosts following him; but when he could run no more, he looked back and realized the sound was only the rain dripping from tree branches onto the leaves spread over the forest floor.

As sunset approached, the rain stopped and the sky cleared. The hunter found what shelter he could under a fallen tree. He tried to sleep, but voices gathered around him and whistled, *"Hyu! hyu! hyu!"* though he could see no one. When the moon rose, the voices scattered like leaves in the wind and left only silence behind. He pulled his blanket over his head and tried again to sleep.

When the hunter awoke the next morning, he decided to go deeper into the woods. But though he found plentiful signs of game all around, he was unable to see a single deer or elk. Disappointed, when night came he found a small clearing and built a fire to warm himself. He ate a bit of *wasna,* then leaned back against a tree trunk to smoke some of the tobacco his father had given him.

He had only taken a puff or two when an old man, wrapped in a red robe, appeared at the edge of the clearing, making the sign of peace. The hunter invited him to sit, and the old man settled down on the other side of the clearing.

The young man, happy to have human company, offered the other some *wasna.* The old man refused, but he asked eagerly for some of his tobacco. The hunter held his pipe out to the other; but when the old man took it and held it by the stem, the younger man saw in the firelight that his fingers were nothing but bones.

Then the stranger let his robe slip back from his shoulders, and all his fleshless ribs were visible. The ghost (for the hunter knew this is what the old man was) did not open his lips when he pulled on the pipe; the smoke came pouring out through his ribs.

When he had finished smoking, the ghost said, "Ho! Now we must wrestle. If I throw you, you will go home empty-handed, to face cold death this winter. If you can throw me, you will catch more game than you can carry, and your family will stay well fed and healthy until the spring."

Since there was nothing else he could do, the young man agreed. But first he threw an armful of brush on the fire; then he put even more brush near the flames.

The ghost rushed at the hunter. He seized him with his bony hands, which hurt the young man painfully, though he did not cry out. Then he tried to push off the ghost, but the skeleton's legs were very powerful, and were locked around the hunter's own.

With great effort, the hunter was able to twist nearer the fire. When the ghost came near it, he grew weak. But when

he was able to pull the young man back toward the darkness, he became strong again.

As the fire burned low, the ghost's strength grew. The man began to get weary, but the thought of his family slowly starving to death gave him added vigor. He was able to force the ghost near the fire again. Then, with a last effort, the hunter yanked one foot free and pushed the pile of brush into the fire. It blazed up instantly, lighting the whole clearing. The ghost let out an ear-piercing scream, and then his skeletal frame began to crumble, until it was nothing more than a pile of ashes.

But the ghost had spoken the truth. The next day the young man caught all the game he needed—more than enough to provide his family for the long, cold winter ahead.

Brother and Sister

(retold from an African folktale)

There was once a stubborn girl who refused to marry any of the young men who came to ask for her hand. The men offered her father cattle and goats in exchange for his daughter, but the young girl would have none of them. Finally her parents grew angry and said they would marry her to the next suitor who came for her.

Soon after this there was a great dance in the village, and all the young men from other villages came. A very tall and handsome man arrived, wearing a headband of gold. All of the unmarried girls tried to catch his eye—but the young woman who had refused to marry was the first to speak to him. When it came time for dancing, he saw to it that he danced close to her. And she fell in love with him.

Later the young man asked for the daughter's hand in marriage, and her mother and father joyfully agreed.

But during the feasting that followed, while everyone laughed and shouted and ate sugar canes, oranges, bananas, and guavas, the girl's little brother saw that the stranger had a second mouth at the back of his head, which was the sure mark of a demon.

He told his mother what he had seen, but she only said,

"What foolishness to think that this fine young man is evil. You are wicked to make up such a story. Be quiet, and share your sister's happiness."

When he went to his father, his father only said the same thing, adding that he would beat the boy if he made trouble. Nor would any of his friends do anything but laugh at him.

So the wedding was celebrated. After several days, the girl and her new husband set off for his home, which was a great distance away.

But her brother, who was worried because of what he had seen, followed them.

As the couple walked along, the husband asked, "Can you still see the smoke from your parents' village?"

"Yes," his new wife answered.

Then he shrugged and they walked on in silence. A little farther along, he asked, "Can you see the hills behind your parents' home?"

"I can see the tops just above the trees," she said. Then they walked farther still.

At last he said, "Can you see the smoke or the hills that mark your old home?"

"No," she replied, "they have disappeared."

"Then we are in my land." And he brought her to a one-room mud hut. It looked like one of the *madili*, temporary houses her people lived in when they were away from their real homes; but the grass thatch was black with the soot of years. There was no *shamba*, vegetable garden, near it. The hut was surrounded by a *boma*, a fence built of thorn branches, like an enclosure where cattle were kept, with only a single small opening in it for a gate. Far away the girl could hear the sound of a rushing river.

There were only a few poor mats and broken pots inside.

The young wife was very disappointed. But because she loved her husband, she only said, "Have you any green maize or beans or sweet potatoes, so that I can fix a meal for you?" For it was growing very late in the day.

"I will eat soon enough," said her husband.

"But," the girl persisted, "surely you have some *shihango?*"—the roasted meat her people kept on hand for emergencies.

"I will eat very soon," her husband replied. Then he sat in the door of the hut and would say nothing else. She set to work cleaning the place, which seemed as dirty as an animal den. When the shadows lengthened, the man rose suddenly and walked down the path into the woods. His new wife called out to him not to leave her alone or risk the dangers of the forest, but he ignored her. Soon the shadows under the trees swallowed him up.

Now the little brother was hidden at the edge of the woods, watching. He secretly followed the man. In a clearing he saw him beginning to change into a hyena. Then the creature threw back its head and shrieked, and the boy, still hidden, heard answering shrieks from all around. In a moment the boy guessed that his sister had been lured to this place to be eaten by the demon and his forest kin.

So the boy raced back to the hut and told his sister what he had seen. At first she refused to believe him. But her husband's strange actions and the howls of approaching hyenas forced her to believe.

Because they did not dare try to outrun the beasts, they rearranged the thorny branches that made up the *boma,* fence, around the hut, to block the only opening. When the animals reached the hut, they found it completely circled by a wall of thorns. At first the creatures only snarled and padded around the outside of the fence.

Then the demon, who was far larger than any true hyena, sprang over the wall of thorns.

The boy and his sister had hidden in the hut and tied the wooden door shut with strips of hide. But the hyena was hurling itself against the door, and they knew it wouldn't last long. So they climbed out the single small window at the back of the hut and onto the roof, just as the beast burst through the entrance. There they found a low-hanging tree branch just within reach.

"Now we must climb for our lives," the boy said.

His sister boosted him up, because he was lighter. Then, when he was safely lying at length on the branch, he stretched down his hand and helped her up. A moment later the hyena realized what they had done and scrambled onto the roof after them. But the sister and brother climbed high up into the branches of the tree, where the beast could not follow.

Then the creature leapt back over the *boma* with a cry. The other hyenas gathered in a circle around the trunk of the tree. Led by the demon, with their powerful jaws they made short work of chewing through the tree.

But the boy and his sister fled to another tree, just as the trunk of the first was bitten through, so it toppled with a *crash*.

As quickly as they reached a new tree, the hyenas began biting its trunk to pieces, so they were forced to flee again. This went on until just before dawn, they came to a tree that grew beside the fast-flowing river. To the right and left there were no trees close enough or big enough to help them. And the beasts had bitten halfway through the last tree.

"Now we must swim," cried the boy.

Before his sister could say anything, the tree fell into the swift river with a *splash*.

They began swimming for the far shore. Snarling, the demon hyena plunged into the water after them. The remaining animals, howling and snapping, ran up and down along the bank, but wouldn't go into the water.

"We can't both get away!" gasped the girl. "I will let him catch me, and you can escape."

"We're almost to the shore!" her brother answered. "Keep swimming."

Just as they reached the sandy bank, the dawn began to break, and the demon turned back into human form. Now it was the tall young man who was swimming after them— but his eyes were those of an angry beast, and he growled like a forest creature.

The brother and sister began throwing rocks at him, so that he could not land. He bellowed at them and threatened them, but they just kept pelting him, so he couldn't get near.

When he began to tire, he turned and swam back toward the other shore.

But the current was too strong and fast for him in his weakened state, and he was carried away and drowned.

Then the boy and girl returned home, where they were welcomed happily by their parents. The little boy was called a hero, and the tale of their terrifying adventure became well known throughout the land.

The Lovers of Dismal Swamp

(United States—Virginia)

There is a swamp in Virginia with an open stretch of water at its very heart. Some people call this Drummond's Pond, but it's also known as the Lake of the Dismal Swamp.

For almost two hundred years, folks say, it has been haunted by two sad ghosts. And this is their story:

The daughter of a family that had settled near the marsh contracted swamp fever. For days she lingered, while the young man who planned to marry her sat by her bedside, holding her hand tightly. By never letting go, he seemed to think that he could hang onto her life, which was slowly slipping away.

But she died and was buried on the edge of the swamp. The young man was so grief-stricken that he refused to go to the funeral. For days he refused to eat or sleep; nor would he listen to any words of comfort. After much pleading, his family and friends convinced him to begin taking care of himself, and he did recover a measure of health. But his mind was never the same.

He began to fancy that his bride-to-be was not dead, but

had merely wandered into the silent, shadowy depths of Dismal Swamp. "She's waiting for me there," he told his friends. "She's hiding because she knew Death was looking for her."

Later his family heard him mutter, "I'll go and find her. And if Old Death comes looking for her, I'll hide her in the hollow of a cypress tree until he goes away."

The young man's family feared that he might harm himself, so they kept him confined to the house and watched him day and night, to keep him from going off to look for his lost love. But one day he slipped away and ran into the swamp.

For a time he heard his father and brothers and friends calling his name as they searched for him. But he only plunged farther into the marsh. Finally the sounds of pursuit were swallowed up in the distance, and the silence of Dismal Swamp all around him was broken only by the cry of a waterbird or the splash of a frog and the persistent buzz of insects.

For days he wandered, eating berries, sleeping on hillocks of dank grass or curled in the roots of trees. His face and hands and clothes were torn by brambles; his boots were caked with mud; several times he narrowly avoided a run-in with a poisonous water snake that slithered over the wet earth.

At last he reached Drummond's Pond late one evening. A will-o'-the-wisp hovered over the surface of the water, far out from shore.

"There she is," he told himself. As he stared through the falling darkness at the bobbing light, he cried excitedly, "I see her! She's standing there holding a lantern!"

Quickly he began gathering together fallen cypress boughs to fashion into a raft. When the flimsy craft was

ready, he launched it onto the water, using a long tree limb stripped of its leaves to pole toward the center of the pond.

He was sure he could see his girl, floating so her feet rested lightly on the black surface of the lake, smiling at him. In her right hand she held a lantern high like a pale beacon to guide him; with her left hand she beckoned him to join her.

"I'm coming, darling!" he called and shoved the long pole even deeper into the murky depths. But his eagerness and a sudden wind that swept across the water, raising waves, undid him. The hastily built raft came apart, and he sank, splashing and crying out his love's name into the dark water, never to rise again.

But hunters who have found themselves near Drummond's Pond when the sun is setting claim to have seen a ghostly raft drifting quietly over the black waters. At the front sits the wraith of a young girl, holding a lantern that gives off pale light. Behind her is a ghastly young man, who poles them along as they vainly search for a way out of Dismal Swamp.

Boneless

(based on folklore of the Shetland Islands)

For a long time people in the Shetland Islands told stories about a creature they could only call "Boneless," or simply, "It," because no two people who had encountered it ever saw quite the same thing. When asked to describe it, one person said it looked like a large jellyfish, another said it was like a lump of wet, white wool, a third said it looked like a pale animal without legs, while a fourth described it as a ghastly white human body without any head. Yet for all that people often claimed it had no legs, it could move faster than a dog; some swore it could fly faster than a hawk, even without wings.

It was most often seen around Christmas time, when the nights are the longest, and goblins and other strange creatures have the greatest power to plague people.

There was a certain farm that "It" troubled every year at Yuletide. The creature would frighten the animals in the barn and make its presence known to everyone in the house, frightening the children and servants so that they huddled in terror all Christmas Eve. Sometimes the farmer or his wife would catch a glimpse of something milk-white and wet as a fishbelly pressed up against the window of the kitchen or the parlor. But it would be gone in the blink of an eye, so that neither could say for sure what he or she had seen.

As a result of this mischief, everyone was so tired and cross the next morning that Christmas Day was ruined. The inhabitants of the farmhouse spent the short day napping and dreading the early onset of night, when the thing would come to haunt them again.

One Christmas Eve, however, the farmer vowed to his wife, "I'll not put up with this again. When 'Boneless' comes, I'll chase it away for good and all."

His wife pleaded with him not to risk angering "It." The thing hadn't hurt anyone, it just gave them the frights. But if her husband made it angry, she reasoned, who knew what such an "unnatural creature" might do?

But her husband's mind was made up. When evening came, he asked his wife to gather the children and servants in the dining room, with the curtain drawn, while he sat in the parlor, reading a Bible by the light of a candle. An axe rested against the leg of his chair.

Toward midnight, he was suddenly alarmed by a sound like a huge mass of wet meat slapped against the front door. Snatching up his Bible in one hand and his axe in the other, he yanked open the door and rushed out.

There was a pool of wetness gleaming on the doorstep in the moonlight, but nothing else. Far down the road he saw something pale like a puddle of moonlight and large as a calf, moving down the road toward the cliffs that overlooked the sea. With a shout of triumph, he chased after the thing.

Just as "It" was about to slip over a cliff and escape into the sea, the farmer shouted, "The Good Lord guide my hand!" and hurled his axe, which stuck fast in the slimy creature. After that, the thing made no movement or sound.

Not daring to go any closer on his own, the man ran back home, where he gathered his servants and persuaded them to accompany him to the spot. There "Boneless" was, like some large pudding, with the axe still sticking in it.

"What's to be done with it now?" asked one young man.

"Bury it," said the farmer, shaking now that the deed was done.

So the men fetched shovels and hastily began to fling earth over the carcass. None of them could tell what it looked like; as they worked to bury it, they got into arguments, because the creature looked different to each pair of eyes. Some were not sure if it was truly dead; and no one, not even the farmer himself, would go near enough to recover the axe. So the tool was buried along with "It."

When no trace of the creature could be seen, they dug a wide trench around the mound of earth, so that neither man nor beast would disturb it. But in fact the people of the neighborhood never went near the spot after that.

In the spring, however, a visitor to the island, who had stopped for the night at the farmhouse, heard the story, and eagerly asked the farmer and his wife for details. Believing it only a local superstition, but curious nonetheless, the stranger went to the mound the next day. He found a part of the ditch wall had collapsed, so that it was easy enough to scramble across to the heap of earth.

Digging with his hands to find out what lay hidden in it, he suddenly saw a thick, curdled light gathering in the hollow he had scooped out. This turned suddenly to a milky mist that gathered around him, dense as a fog from the sea, but pale as if steeped in moonlight (though it was still midday).

Frightened, he backed away from the mound and hurried across the crumbling earth to the other side of the ditch.

He had just reached safety there when *something* rose out of the hole, rolled across the trench, and vanished into the mist in the direction of the ocean.

By the time the visitor had reached the farmhouse, the strange, milk-white mist had become an ordinary gray fog, and he had calmed down somewhat. He was sure that what he had seen was something quite natural which had just appeared unnatural because he had been more frightened by the stories of strange creatures than he wanted to admit.

"Surely what I saw was nothing more than an otter or a seal," he said, "something that happened to be near the mound when I chanced to be there."

But the farmer merely shook his head. "We all know there's many kinds of life that live in the air, on the earth, or in the water. And we, poor mortals, have not the power to understand the like of some of them."

The stranger did not get into an argument with his host, though he thought the man a superstitious bumpkin and was angry at himself for believing, even for a moment, such a story.

Two nights later the traveler, who had become somewhat lost, was hiking along a stretch of road high above a cove. He had just located the pinpoints of light that marked the village he was seeking and was heading toward it. He could hear waves breaking on the rocks far below him. Suddenly in the moonlight, he saw something long and white stretched across the road. It wasn't fog, though it had a wet, kind of misty look to it. He couldn't see the lights of the distant town any longer.

The whiteness began to slither toward him, as if it were

alive. Without hesitating, he turned and began to run back the way he'd come. But the thing overtook him in an instant. It wrapped itself around him so that he felt like he was being smothered in a heavy, wet blanket. It was as cold as if it had been soaked in the night sea, and smelled of rotten fish.

Then he felt his waist, legs, and ankles caught in nooses like an octopus's tentacles. His bonds glowed like ropes of moonlight, but were tough as the hardiest seaweed. They began dragging him toward the cliff edge, the ocean below, and certain death.

He tried to call for help; but he was so scared, the sound caught in his throat, as surely as if an assassin's cord had tightened around his neck. He scrambled for a claw hold on the stony path, but his fingernails scraped and slid over the hard rocks without giving him any purchase.

Just as he felt his feet, his knees, then his thighs being yanked over the edge of the cliff—in the instant before he tumbled off into the hungry darkness—he managed to hook his left arm around a sharp outcropping of rock. He flung his right arm around it also, and hung on for dear life. From this dizzying perch, he dared to look below him.

Half of him dangled into space, lassoed by silvery ropes stretching down into the darkness, twisting together into a single cable that linked him to a luminous splotch in the waves hundreds of feet below.

The deadly ropes pulled tighter. He tightened his grip on the rock in response. He had the sickening feeling that he might be torn in two if he—or the horrible thing that had him in thrall—didn't let go.

"Oh, sweet Lord," he prayed—

—and felt the thing loosen its grasp, just a little.

He recalled how the farmer had used a Bible and a

prayer to help defeat the thing once. *A prayer, a prayer,* he told himself, *I need a prayer.*

But in his fright, he could remember nothing except a prayer he had said as a child:

> "Now I lay me down to sleep,
> I pray the Lord my soul to keep;
> If I should die before I wake,
> I pray the Lord—"

At the second mention of "the Lord," the loops of moonlight loosened, then dropped away.

Looking below, he saw ribbons of light coiling down, hitting the churning waves with a sizzle like a candle flame extinguished in a saucer of water.

For an instant, circles of cold fire spread outward, one after the other like ripples in a pond. Then all the light was gone. There was only the empty black surf pounding below him.

Painfully he climbed back onto the road, where he lay for a long time, just catching his breath.

When he reached the town, the traveler was too shaken to do anything more than ask when the earliest boat was leaving for the mainland. He left the next day for London, never to return to Shetland.

The Death Waltz

(United States—New Mexico)

In 1851, when New Mexico was still a territory and had not yet become a state, Fort Union was built ninety miles northeast of Santa Fe, to protect people from Apache Indian raids. The fort helped keep the trails open, so that huge, red-wheeled freight wagons, pulled by teams of mules or yokes of oxen, could bring hardware, calico, and other goods to Santa Fe, while taking furs, hides, and Mexican mules and burros back to St. Louis, Missouri.

Fort Union was the only spot for miles around where an effort was made to keep up the appearances of gracious social life, such as was found east of the Missouri River. There were a number of very beautiful young ladies attached to the post, and the most attractive of them all was Elizabeth Bidwell, the sister-in-law of Captain Moore. She had recently come to Fort Union to stay with her sister, the captain's wife, because their parents were dead, and the maiden aunt who had raised Elizabeth had become ill.

Young Elizabeth enjoyed the excitement that came from living on an outpost where the threat of an Indian attack lurked always in the background. She was doubly delighted by the attentions the young officers paid to her, since there were few women who were both pretty and unmarried in that wild country.

One lieutenant named Frank Sutter, recently transferred from the east, was especially attracted to Elizabeth's charms. He devoted himself to winning her hand, in spite of the other handsome officers who buzzed around her like bees discovering the sweetest blossom in a garden.

Frank Sutter's experience with the world was not large enough so that he could tell whether a woman was responding seriously to his attentions or was merely flirting with him. He would walk with Elizabeth in the afternoon, when the sunny, clear air would turn in the blink of an eye to heavy rain that sent them scurrying for cover—then disappeared as quickly as it had begun to fall. They would sit together in the evening, watching the sky turn red, pink, orange, and yellow to the west, while the mountains to the east of the fort turned dark, purple, mysterious.

At such times, Frank would talk to Elizabeth about many things—but he didn't dare tell the young woman, whose hand rested lightly on his arm, just what he felt for her.

Elizabeth laughed, and fanned herself, and complained about the heat, and chattered on about how bored she was growing with life at Fort Union and how eager she was to return to Missouri and the social life there. Such talk cut Lieutenant Sutter to the quick, but he never let his pain show.

Then one day, messengers came racing to the fort with news of a series of Apache raids. Captain Moore ordered a detachment of troops to chase and punish the guilty Indians. Lieutenant Sutter was put in command of the expedition.

The night before they were to set out, however, he called on Elizabeth Bidwell. Drawing her to a private corner of the porch, he dropped to his knee and said, "Elizabeth, if you didn't guess it before, I'm telling you now: I'm in love with you."

She smiled at him, then turned her head away and patted her heart. Finally she said, "Why, Lieutenant Sutter, I'm *overwhelmed* by the honor you're giving me."

"And do you have some affection for me?"

"You don't even have to ask," she replied, blushing.

"Then, Miss Bidwell, will you do me the honor of marrying me when I return?"

He was the handsomest young officer in Fort Union, and his prospects were excellent. Elizabeth answered without thought or hesitation, "Of course I will."

"But, if the fortunes of war deprive me of life—"

"Hush!" she said, "Don't even think such a thing! If you should fail to return, I *swear* I will never marry another."

"Then," he said, rising to his feet and kissing her hand, "you can be assured nobody else will have you. I will come back and make my claim."

The lieutenant and his troops departed the next morning. On the evening of their second day on patrol, they overtook the band of Apaches that had gone on the warpath. In the heat of battle, Frank Sutter became separated from the rest of his men. When the dust had settled and the Indians had scattered into the dusk, the troops searched vainly for the young lieutenant, but he had vanished. When they could turn up no trace of him, they returned to Fort Union and reported him missing in action.

Other people at the fort noted (not very kindly) that Elizabeth Bidwell, Frank Sutter's bride-elect, grieved very little for the missing bridegroom-to-be. And it came as no great surprise to anyone when she announced her intention of marrying a man recently arrived from the East, who would take her back to St. Louis with him.

Her sister and brother-in-law arranged a wedding for her on the post. When the big day arrived, there was a short ceremony in the chapel; then everyone retired in the evening to the mess hall, which was decorated for a ball.

Outside a sudden thunderstorm rolled through nearby canyons, and sent rain splatting against the roof and walls of the mess hall. But inside all was festivity: there was good food, lots to drink, and loud laughter everywhere. A band was playing with more enthusiasm than tunefulness, but everyone was having a fine time. At the heart of everything was Elizabeth Bidwell, smiling and fanning herself and swirling her skirts of roseblush pink.

Suddenly, when the dance was at full swing, the outside doors of the hall slammed open with a *bang*, letting in a draught of air that made the candles gutter and burn low.

A bloodcurdling cry, neither human nor like any other bird or creature anyone could name, echoed through the common room, carried on the invading wind. All eyes turned to the open doorway. Framed by the doorposts was the body of a dead man, dressed in the stained uniform of a cavalry officer. Across his forehead was a gash left by a tomahawk. His eyes were wide open and burned with a fiery light.

As everyone retreated to the edges of the dance floor, the horrible apparition walked across the floor to the new bride, and pulled her from the arms of her husband. Like the rest of the company, she stood gaping, too shocked to move. The corpse led Elizabeth to the center of the floor; she moved as stiffly as a doll, her mouth working but no sound coming out. Suddenly the thing that had been Lieutenant Sutter clasped the young woman closely to him. Then he gave a signal to the musicians.

Afterward the shaken men protested that they did not know what they were doing. But at the corpse's command, they began to play a waltz, so strange and haunting in its melody that some people burst into tears upon hearing it, while others pressed their hands to their ears to keep out the sound.

On the floor the couple whirled around and around and around. Elizabeth could not take her gaze from the dead lieutenant's burning eyes, but she grew paler and paler. The musicians, possessed by some compulsion from beyond the grave, played faster and faster, until the music became so frantic that the spinning couple out on the floor became a blur of pink skirts and blue uniform.

Then the music slowed from a pace that no human could dance to, back to a waltz, and down to a dirge. The young woman hung limply in the corpse's arms; her slack jaw and empty eyes showed that she was as dead as her partner.

Gently the dead man lowered her body to the floor. For a moment he stood staring down at her; then his eyes circled the horrified company. He threw back his head and gave the same fearful cry they had heard earlier. Then he turned and marched stiffly out into the driving wind and rain, while the doors of the mess hall slammed shut behind him.

When people could move again, Elizabeth's bridegroom rushed to her side, but his efforts to revive her were futile.

The corpse had vanished into the storm that battered Fort Union for a day and a night.

Several days later a troop of soldiers which had been sent to the scene of the earlier battle located Frank Sutter's body where it lay at the bottom of a small gulley, with a single tomahawk gash across the forehead.

He was returned to the post and buried beside Elizabeth Bidwell, in the little cemetery outside the fort.

The Ghost of Misery Hill

(United States—California)

There was once a miner, Tom Bowers, who worked a claim on Misery Hill, near Pike City, in California. Tom was a loner: he never liked having people around him, he only went into town when he needed supplies, and he never took a partner. "Nobody's going to work my claim but *me!*" he told anyone who offered to buy into his claim.

During the winter he laid in supplies and kept to himself, while the snowdrifts piled up high around his cabin. People in Pike City always knew spring had arrived when Tom came down from Misery Hill to purchase a fresh batch of foodstuffs.

But one spring, long after the last traces of snow had melted, the inhabitants of Pike City noticed that Old Tom hadn't turned up with his poke of gold dust to buy beans and salt pork, bread and coffee. After a good deal of discussion, a group of miners and townspeople rode off to investigate.

They found Tom's cabin empty; the pot-bellied stove was stone cold, and some bits of fried bread had gone moldy in the big iron skillet on top of it. Clearly no one had been in the one-room shack for a long time.

Certain now that something had happened to the old miner, the men followed the path that ran from his cabin to the brink of the steep slope where he had done his prospecting. But they found the end of the trail had vanished—had been blotted out by a huge landslide.

Fearing the worst, they dug into the pile of earth and rock; and, after half a day of hard work, they found the old man's body. Then, having solved the mystery and having nothing better to do with Tom's remains, they buried him properly in a shallow grave not far from the mouth of his old mine shaft.

A few miners thought to work Tom's mine on Misery Hill, but the story soon grew that the ghost of Tom Bowers was often seen prowling around, carrying his old pick, near his mine. Soon everybody avoided the spot.

There was one miner, Jim Brandon, who got himself so far into debt when his own claim ran out that he became desperate. He moved into Tom's long-empty shack and began to work the abandoned mine. Soon enough he made it pay well enough to clear up his debts and accumulate a nest egg for himself.

But after several months, he began to notice signs that someone else was working his claim by night. Every morning he could see that somebody had tampered with the sluice—a long wooden trough he filled every day with freshly dug gravel. When water from a nearby stream was run down it, bars along the bottom of the sluice would catch any gold the gravel might hold.

Jim searched high and low for a clue to his midnight visitor but found nothing. Thinking some of the other miners might be playing a trick on him, he challenged them. But they all swore they knew nothing about it.

After this, things were quiet for a few days. Then one morning, Jim again found that someone had been loading the sluice with gravel and running water through it. When evening came, he loaded his rifle and, hiding himself in a nook from which he had a clear view of the claim site, he kept watch for the intruder.

For a long time he heard nothing but the wind whistling through the pines, and the Yuba River rushing over rocks nearby. He could see the distant ridges of the Sierras gleaming in the starlight, but though he strained his eyes, he saw nothing moving near the mine entrance.

Then, by the light of the newly risen moon, he saw a notice shining on a nearby tree trunk, as though someone had just tacked it into place. Curious, he walked over and found the odd sign was as easy to read as if it was glowing by itself, not just reflecting the light of the full moon. It said,

Notice!
I, Tom Bowers
Claim this ground
for placer mining.

Sure now that he was the victim of practical jokers, Jim grabbed for the paper to tear it down—only to feel an electric jolt run from his fingertips to his shoulder. His arm fell numbly at his side.

The notice vanished.

At the same time there came to his ears the sound of gravel being dumped into the sluice. A moment later he heard water gurgling into it, then the rattling and bumping of rocks being tumbled down the length of it.

Shaking his arm back into use, he angrily grabbed his gun and headed toward the sluice. Out of the corner of his eye, he saw the message was glowing again on the tree trunk, but he ignored it. He heard the sound of a pick biting into gravel, now, and nothing mattered except finding out what was going on.

Leveling his rifle, he rounded an outcrop of rock and saw Tom Bowers, swinging his pick near the entrance to the mine. The miner turned to glare at Jim, and the frightened man saw at a glance that he was a ghost. Tom's tall, skinny frame glowed just like the notice on the tree. His head and face were half-covered, with lank, white hair; his eyes blazed from black sockets.

Scared nearly out of his wits, Jim raised his rifle to his shoulder and fired.

The gun's report was followed by a bellow from Tom's ghost. Looking through the rifle smoke, Jim saw the spectre charging at him, his pick raised in both his hands.

"Oh, *Lordy!*" cried Jim and, still clutching his rifle, he took off running, with the angry ghost only a few paces behind.

The living led the dead a wild chase up hill and down, into and out of woods, over streams and ditches, and through scrub, toward Pike City.

In town the miners were all gathered in the saloon, celebrating a new gold strike. Suddenly everyone froze when they heard an ear-splitting scream. Then there was a sound like a body falling, followed by the clang of metal hitting on metal—then silence.

Everyone tumbled outside to see what had happened.

In the middle of the road, they found Jim Brandon's rifle pinned to the ground by the point of a pick sunk clean through the barrel. On the pick's handle were carved the initials "T.B."

No one ever saw Jim Brandon after that night. But for years afterward, miners working near Misery Hill reported the sluice at Tom Bowers's claim ran every night, just like clockwork.

The Loup-Garou (The Werewolf)

(from French-Canadian folklore)

In the old time in Canada, people believed the werewolf, which they called the *loup-garou,* haunted grave-yards and prowled the woods and waited in the brush beside lonely trails to catch unwary travelers and gobble them up.

There was an old couple living on a farm far out in the country. One wintry night Marthe took very ill, and her husband, Pierre, had to go to fetch the doctor in town. This meant a long, long journey through the woods. But Pierre was too worried about his wife to hesitate. He hitched up his horse to his sleigh and set out through the lightly falling snow.

As he went along, he could hear nothing except the *scrunch, scrunch* of snow under the sleigh's runners and the horse's hoofs. The old man wasn't thinking of anything except getting help for Marthe as fast as he could.

They were now a long way into the woods. Moonlight shone on the snow, which lay thick on the ground and on branches of the pine trees all around. Sometimes from deep in the shadows would come the sharp report of an ice-heavy branch snapping and dropping to the ground. Once, Pierre heard an owl hooting. Except for these sounds, silence lay heavily over the forest.

The road ahead was level and easy enough for the horse. But suddenly the animal began to slow down. Pierre shook the reins and shouted, "Giddup!" but the horse was hardly moving at all now. It was as if he was pulling a two-ton load, rather than the little sleigh with its single passenger. The old man flicked his whip, but the horse merely shook its head and made a frightened little whinney. The poor animal was breathing rapidly, his warm breath making clouds like the steam from a steamboat's chimney; sweat was running down his flank.

Now Pierre could feel some of the horse's fear sinking into him. Then there was a low growl just behind him that stood his hair on end. Turning, he discovered what looked like a great big black dog or wolf, its teeth and the claws of its forepaws sunk into the back of the sleigh, its hindpaws dragging on the ground, bringing the sled nearly to a halt.

For one terrible moment Pierre stared directly into the creature's burning yellow eyes. Then, almost without thinking, he cracked his whip across the monster's snout. The wolf gave a howl of pain and loosened its hold on the sleigh for a moment. In that instant the horse lunged forward and ran as if all the devils from hell were in pursuit.

Looking over his shoulder, Pierre could see the shadowy creature bounding down the road close behind. The man knew that unless his guardian angel was riding with him that night, it was all over for him.

He didn't need to urge the horse to go faster: the animal was so scared that he galloped like a hurricane. But for all that, the monster was getting closer.

And closer.

And—

The creature gave a tremendous leap and landed on the back of the sleigh. The *thump* of the impact and the sudden weight on the end of the sleigh sent it sliding first to one side of the road then the other. For a moment Pierre thought he was going to crash; but miraculously the sleigh kept upright on its runners and found the center of the road again. The horse, now crazy with fear, somehow managed to keep from falling in the icy road, often blocked with drifts of snow.

The wolf was growling as it crept toward the old man, who had turned to face the beast. Pierre tried using his whip again, but the monster caught it in his huge jaws, severing it as if it was no more than a twig and tossing it over the edge of the wildly careening sleigh.

Old Pierre felt for his hunting knife, and pulled it free, just as the wolf sprang at him and slammed the man to the bottom of the sleigh. His forepaws were on Pierre's shoulders, pinning him to the floorboards; the man felt his bones were likely to break under the weight of the monster. For one terrible instant he felt the creature's whiskers brush his face like needles, felt its hot breath on his throat, saw its yellow eyes only inches from his own—

Then, with a prayer, he jabbed at the thing with his hunting knife. Though his movement was hampered by the weight of the monster on top of him, he managed to nick it just enough to draw blood, so a spot of red appeared on its pelt.

Instantly the creature reared back, howling like nothing Pierre had ever heard before; then, to the old man's astonishment, the wolf turned into a man. Right away, Pierre knew that this was, indeed, a *loup-garou,* because the stories say if you draw blood from the *loup-garou,* he'll turn back to a man right off and run away.

Pressing his big, pale hand to his side, the man suddenly

leapt off the sleigh. Pierre saw him rolling down a hillside through the snow, where the forest shadows quickly hid him.

Then the sleigh was out of the woods and heading toward the sleeping town ahead. Shaking, Pierre returned his knife to its holster and took hold of the reins, gradually easing the horse back to a trot, saying, "Easy, easy."

When they reached the gate of the doctor's house, Pierre quickly roused the man, who thought at first the old man was the one who was sick, because he was so pale and trembling. But when Pierre told what had happened, the doctor gave him a shot of whiskey. Then they roused the village priest, who gave them holy water and a cross as protection for their journey back through the woods.

Pierre never saw the *loup-garou* again. But Marthe, when she recovered, made him promise never to travel through the woods alone at night again, and the old man was only too happy to give her his word that he never would.

The Golem

(based on Jewish folklore)

There was a rich merchant who lived in a city in Eastern Europe in the sixteenth century. He had heard of the golem, a manlike creature fashioned out of clay that Rabbi Elijah of Chelm and Rabbi Yehuda Loew of Prague had created to serve them. Desiring such a servant for himself, the merchant went to his friend the rabbi, who was a wise man. The good rabbi had studied the magical books of the Kabbala and had discovered many secrets that had been hidden from men's eyes since the beginning of time.

And the most wonderful—and terrible—thing he discovered was how to create a golem. After much persuading, the merchant got the rabbi to agree to bring such a creature to life. The rich man fashioned the likeness of a man out of yellow clay his servants fetched up from the riverbank. He lovingly shaped the hands and feet and head, and carefully sculpted a human face. Then the rabbi said magic formulas from the *Book of Creation* over the figure, walked around it seven times, and wrote the Hebrew word *Emet*, which means "Truth," on the creature's forehead.

Instantly the clay body turned red as fire, and the creature came to life. Hair sprouted on its head, and nails

appeared on its fingers and toes. It climbed clumsily to its feet and stood watching the two men. The rabbi stood for a long time looking at his handiwork and stroking his beard. At last, without saying a word, he left the rich man's house.

The merchant was delighted to have the perfect servant, who would never tire, needed nothing to eat or drink, would require no pay—and could not even complain, because the power that had brought him to life did not give him the power of speech. He ordered the golem to draw water from the well and sweep the courtyard. Silently the clay man went about his tasks.

And for a time he proved an admirable servant. But each day the golem grew a little bit taller and broader, and slower to take the merchant's orders.

Still he was a tireless worker. And when he had grown bigger, the rich man sent him to carry goods to nearby towns and fetch back items the merchant needed for his own business, which prospered. Soon he became the richest man in the city.

When he walked out in the afternoon, the golem trudged silently behind him, to frighten off robbers who might come for his gold or shoo away beggars who also wanted some of his money. No one, looking at the tall, hulking guard of red clay would dream of making the merchant angry.

And still the golem grew a little bit more each day; and each day, the merchant saw in the creature's eyes something that made him uncomfortable, though he could not give it a name.

He asked his friend the rabbi about this, but the old scholar merely shrugged and said, "I can bring the clay to life; I can tell you how to destroy it; more I cannot say."

"I will never destroy my servant," said the merchant, "I am a man of real position now. People tremble when they see me coming; they make way when they hear my servant's footstep on the street."

Soon the golem was nearly twice the height and bulk of a man. In the evening, when the merchant sat at his table, being waited on by the clay figure, he would sometimes grow oddly uneasy as the creature shuffled back and forth to the kitchen. The glow from the fireplace would sometimes light his servant's face in such a way that the thing seemed to watch him with a look of anger. At such moments he was glad that his friend the rabbi had not been able to give the golem the power of speech.

The man's other servants ran away, frightened of the golem. But now the creature was so big it did the work of several, and the merchant could command it to labor all through the night, while he slept—so he counted himself better off. His friends would no longer come to visit, but he was so absorbed with the demands of his growing business that he hardly noticed.

Still the golem grew. Now it had to stoop to enter by even the great front doors of the merchant's house. And the merchant sometimes had to tell his clay servant several times over to do even the simplest task. One morning he had to scream until he was nearly hoarse before the golem took up the broom to sweep and a bucket to clean the ashes from the hearth.

When he returned in the afternoon, he found the broom snapped in half in the middle of the floor and the pail crushed and tossed into the ashes of the fireplace. Angrily the merchant shouted for his servant, but the golem did not come. The man searched all the rooms of the house, but found no trace of the creature.

He went outside, and found the clay being, which was now twice as tall as the tallest man, standing in a far corner of the garden. He ordered the golem to return to the house and finish the tasks he had started, but the thing only stood looking down at him. Something in the way it stared at him made the man take first one and then another step back.

The merchant made one last attempt to regain control of matters. "Since you're out here already," he said, mustering as much authority as he could, "you can draw water from the well for the evening meal."

He was relieved to see the golem start for the well. But instead of drawing water, the creature began to smash the well to bits. Then it turned and began uprooting the fruit trees in the garden.

The merchant tried in vain to get it to stop. But the red clay figure, now almost as high as the wall surrounding the garden, continued its work of destruction, moving closer to the house. Frantic, the man ran about, ordering the creature to stop. But the golem no longer heard him—or if it heard, it no longer would obey.

Terrified, the rich man ran through the rooms of his house, calling for help, but his servants were long gone and no one else dared come near the place. Behind him, he heard splintering wood and a sound like stone grinding on stone. Afraid for his very life, he ran out into the street and hurried to the home of his friend the rabbi.

"Tell me what to do to stop the golem!" he shouted, as soon as he entered his friend's study.

Startled, the rabbi asked what had happened, and the man quickly explained.

"You must erase the first letter from the word *Emet*, which is written on the golem's forehead," the rabbi said. "Then the word becomes *met*, 'death,' and the creature will cease to exist."

The man hurried back home, to find the huge clay figure rampaging through the house, pulling down curtains, smashing holes in the walls, breaking the elegant furnishings into kindling. Seeing his home in ruins, the merchant cried in a loud voice, *"Stop!"*

This time, the golem obeyed. It halted in the center of the room, looking at its master. After a few moments, when he was convinced he again had control of the creature, the merchant dared to come closer. He looked at the word *Emet* written on the golem's forehead, but it was now quite out of reach, because the monster had grown so tall.

The creature waited, staring down at the man.

"I have some things you must do," the merchant began, letting his voice grow softer with each word, "but I have so worn my voice out that I can only whisper what you are to do." Now his voice was little more than a whisper itself: "Bend down and hear my commands."

Stiffly the golem leaned down toward its master. As soon as he could reach its forehead, the merchant rubbed out the *E,* turning *Emet* to *met,* "Truth" to "death."

At that moment, the golem broke apart. But the lifeless mass of yellow clay it once again became fell and crushed the merchant to death.

Lavender

(United States)

Not so long ago, two college freshmen were driving along the road one evening on their way to a dance at a neighboring women's college. Bill, who owned the sleek red convertible, was driving slowly because the road was unfamiliar. Eric, who had a roadmap unfolded over his lap, said, "We're sure not on the highway any longer. We made a wrong turn back there somewhere."

"You're one lousy navigator," laughed Bill, "but what the heck! We're taking the scenic route."

"Yeah," Eric responded, not too enthusiastically, "but I'd just as soon get off this road before it gets too dark." He looked nervously out the car window at the shadows gathering under the trees on either side of the road.

"Hold on!" cried Bill, slamming his foot on the brake. "I think our luck just changed for the better!" He pointed through the windshield to where a slim, young woman stood by the side of the road, flagging them down. In the half-light of evening, they could see she was wearing an old-fashioned lavender dress. Since so many of the women they knew wore old-style clothes they had bought at thrift

shops or antique stores, the young men saw nothing un-
usual in the way the girl dressed.

Bill brought the car to a halt on the dusty shoulder of the
road. "Need a lift?" he called to the attractive young
woman.

"I'm going to a dance at Gabriel College," she answered. "I'd appreciate a ride."

"We're going there ourselves," said Bill. "Why don't you
hop in and come with us?"

"I believe I will," she said and smiled, climbing into the
back seat of the car, while Eric held the door open for her.
He was struck by how pale her face was, and how cold her
hand felt when it brushed his. There was a faint fragrance
of lavender that clung to her, which reminded Eric of his
grandmother. But all he said was, "We're lost: I'm the
world's worst navigator."

"That's fixed easily enough," their passenger said. Then
she gave them careful directions that soon guided them
back to the main highway. The three young people talked
and joked all the way to Gabriel College. Eric forgot his
uneasiness and cracked awful jokes that had Bill groaning.
But the young woman in the back seat laughed as though
he were the world's greatest comedian.

As they were pulling into the parking lot at the college,
Bill suddenly said, "Say, we don't even know your name."

"Oh," she laughed, "just call me 'Lavender,' since that's
my favorite color." Then she pushed open the door of the
car and climbed out. The music of drums and guitars
thrummed across the parking lot. "Hurry," she pleaded,
holding a hand out to Bill and Eric, "I don't want to miss a
moment of this night!"

Bill took her right hand and Eric, her left. The three of
them ran like small children toward the bright lights and
loud music.

Inside, while Eric watched Lavender dance with Bill, he thought, *I could fall in love with someone like her.* Then he felt himself blushing, because he'd never felt that way about anyone before. *And,* he reminded himself, *you don't even know her name.* But the mystery that clung to her like the fragrance of lavender only made her seem that much more alluring. Then it struck him, *I'm already in love with her.* Watching Bill on the dance floor with the beautiful, lavender-gowned girl, he guessed that Bill was falling in love with her, too.

How he would sort this out with his best friend was anybody's guess. But "Lavender" was worth it—of that he had no doubt.

When the dance ended, Bill suggested they go someplace for coffee; but the girl only said, "I have to go home." To Eric, she sounded very, very tired.

Bill protested this, but she simply said, *"Please. I have to go home."* Something in her voice left no room for further argument.

As they crossed the parking lot, she began to shiver. Eric gallantly gave her his sportcoat, and she gratefully wrapped it around her shoulders. But she seemed to shiver just as much. He was tempted to put his arm around her, but something about her made him hold back—for all he cursed himself for being a shy fool.

It was very late when they left the highway and started up the side road where they had first met "Lavender."

With an odd, faraway sound in her voice, she directed them to a run-down shack way at the end of a rutted dirt road. There was a single light burning in one window.

When Eric and Bill offered to walk her to her door, she said quickly, "No, I have to go alone!" Again her tone of voice stopped their objections cold.

She waved once—a graceful lavender shadow in the mingled moonlight and starlight—then hurried toward the lighted window like a moth drawn to a flame. With a sigh Bill popped the car into reverse and headed back down the driveway.

It wasn't until they were almost back to their own campus that Eric said, "Hey! She never gave me back my jacket."

"I wondered when you'd notice," chuckled Bill.

"Why didn't you say something?" Eric demanded.

"Don't worry," laughed Bill, "this gives us an excuse to go back tomorrow, find out her real name, and get to know our mysterious 'Lavender' better."

"Oh, yeah," said Eric, eager for a chance to see the young woman again.

Shortly after noon the next day, Bill and Eric drove up to the cabin at the end of the rutted road. They had to knock several times before a very old woman in a faded housedress answered. She glanced from one to the other with watery eyes.

"We've, um, come to see a young lady who calls herself 'Lavender,' " Bill explained.

The old woman shook her head. "I don't know anybody named 'Lavender,' " she said.

But when Eric described the young woman they had met on the road the evening before, she suddenly pressed trembling fingers to her mouth and whispered, "That was *Lily.*"

"So, where is she?" Bill wanted to know.

"She's been dead for many years," said the old woman, wiping a tear away from her eye. "Lily was my daughter, but she died in a car accident on her way to a dance. She's buried in the cemetery two miles down the road." The woman gave a sigh and dabbed at her eye with a crumpled Kleenex. "You're not the first to see her: she often tries to come home. I leave a light burning all night, every night, just hoping some night she'll make it all the way back to me. But that's never happened."

"But—" Eric started to say.

Bill grabbed him by the arm and steered him back to the car. When he had pushed his friend into the front seat and started the engine, Bill said, "Don't you *see*? It's a joke. She doesn't want to see us anymore, so she put the old woman up to telling that story. We've just been given a brush-off, so let's forget the whole thing."

"But my coat . . ."

"You needed a new one, anyway," said Bill. "I'm not going back to that dump ever again. I know when I've been had!"

They drove for a while in silence. Suddenly Eric shouted, "Stop! Pull over!"

Startled, Bill did as his friend said, bringing the car to a halt outside the walls of a small country cemetery. Before Bill could stop him, Eric had leapt out of the car and run through the rusted iron gates that hung ajar. With a soft curse, Bill shut off the engine and climbed out.

He caught up with Eric as his friend was walking up and down rows of gravestones, reading each.

Abruptly Eric stopped, pointing at a small, white gravestone.

"What . . . ?" Bill began, then he fell silent.

Engraved on the tombstone was the name *Lily Abbott*. The dates inscribed showed that the woman had died more than thirty years before. Lying neatly folded on the grass below the stone was Eric's sportcoat.

"It's a trick," Bill said weakly.

But neither one of them believed it.

The Goblin Spider

(a Japanese legend)

There was once a famous samurai named Raiko, who was sent by the Emperor of Japan to rid the country of a terrible goblin spider plaguing the countryside near the city of Kyoto. This famous warrior went searching for the monster with his companion, Tsuna. When they reached the plain of Rendai, which was supposed to be haunted, the two men suddenly saw a skull floating in the air in front of them.

"Have you come to destroy the spider?" the skull asked.

"We have," answered Raiko.

"The monster killed me many years ago," said the skull. "I have waited a long time to see the beast punished. I will show you where to find it."

Before they could question their ghostly friend any further, the skull flew away in front of them, as though it was driven by the wind. The two knights followed as fast as they could. But when they had almost caught up with their strange guide, it suddenly disappeared.

Looking around them, the two men discovered nearby the ruins of a palace. Entering the littered courtyard through a crumbling archway, they saw a strange old woman, sitting on a broken pillar across from them. She was dressed in white, with lank white hair; her face was a mass of wrinkles, delicate as spiders' webs. When she raised her heavy eyelids, her eyes glittered like an insect's, black and cold, at Raiko and Tsuna.

"Warriors, you are not welcome here," she said to them. "I am two hundred and ninety years old. For all my life I have served the demon who haunts this place. Be warned: if you linger here, the monster will slay you as he has slain countless other men—some as brave as you or as foolish."

"We won't be frightened away," said Tsuna.

"Begone, hag," commanded Raiko, "and tell the creature you serve that we are here by the will of the Emperor, who commands us rid his kingdom of the goblin spider."

At this, the old woman broke into a cackling laugh. "I will send some friends to entertain you, while I tell my mistress you have come to see her."

With that, the hag melted into a pale mist and vanished through a crack in the courtyard flagging. At the same moment, dark storm clouds began to gather above the shattered palace; flashes of lightning lit the ruins all around them. A short time later, rain began to patter onto the flagstones of the court.

"Hsssst!" warned Raiko, grabbing his companion's shoulder. "Listen!"

Now Tsuna could hear it also: ghostly footsteps all around them. Suddenly a great company of demons poured out into the rain: some were huge with horns, three toes, three fingers, and three eyes; some looked like animals but walked like men, with faces that were a horrifying mix of beast and human; one had its eyes in its hands, and kept its palms up so it could see; another was a serpent with a woman's head, its long hair flying and its tongue flickering out to taste the rain; small creatures, like frogs or monkeys with a shock of red hair, pranced around the legs of their taller companions.

Both samurai drew their swords. In an instant the gruesome horde was upon them, but their flashing swords kept the monsters at bay. On and on they fought, while more monsters came from the shadows to join those already battling the two heroes. Toward morning, the rain slackened, and the thunder died away somewhat, but still the demons kept up the attack.

Then, over the sounds of battle and the dying storm, Raiko heard a distant cock crowing.

A shudder ran through the monstrous company surrounding them. When the cock crowed a second time, the hideous creatures began retreating to the shadows of the ruins. Hissing and snarling and screeching, the goblin army fled the approaching dawn.

When they were alone in the vast courtyard, Raiko and Tsuna hugged each other and each complimented the other on his bravery.

Then they heard a single pair of footsteps climbing an unseen staircase. In a doorway on the far side of the courtyard, a beautiful, pale woman dressed in white appeared. She looked as slender and graceful as a willow, curving in the breeze. Silently she beckoned the two men to come nearer.

But when they were close to her, she was suddenly wrapped in a fierce white light, brighter than the sun, which blinded the two men. Tsuna gave a cry, dropped to the ground, and pressed his hands to his eyes. Then he rolled to one side. Raiko turned his head aside and raised his left arm to shield his eyes; with his right arm he drew his sword.

The dazzling light grew fainter by degrees. Looking into it from an angle, Raiko saw that the beautiful woman had become a ghastly creature: a thing with a tiny body and a head two feet long that floated at the end of a reedlike neck. Her arms were white as snow, long and thin as ropes that were snaking out toward the half-blinded warrior.

Just as the awful creature touched him, Raiko shouted and struck at her with his sword. She turned into threads of silk that disappeared down between the stones of the courtyard, just as the old hag had vanished earlier. Raiko found that he was covered with cobwebs as thick as wire. As he pulled the sticky strands off, Tsuna, who had also recovered from the blinding, joined his friend. Together they discovered that Raiko's sword was smeared with *white* blood.

The sun had returned now; the last of the rainwater was seeping away through the cracks between the flagstones.

After watching this for a while, Raiko clashed his sword on the stone several times, then said, "There is a vast hollow space below us. That is where the hag and the other creature fled. Surely that is where the goblin spider has its den."

"There must be a way down through the building," suggested Tsuna.

"To be sure," said Raiko. "But the monster must fear the sunlight, or else it would have come after us itself—not sent others to warn us away. We would be smart to bring the sun with us."

"How?" asked Tsuna.

"Like this," said Raiko, and he sank the point of his sword between two flagstones and pried one loose. The ancient mortar crumbled easily; stone after stone came free and was tossed into a far corner of the courtyard.

Suddenly from the shadowy depths below, a voice cried, "Stop! The sunlight burns me! Go away, I grant you your lives."

But the two men only worked harder, revealing a vast room under the courtyard. Peering into the spot where the shadows were deepest, Raiko saw a monster with many legs, covered with long, silky white hair. It had an enormous head, split with terrible jaws, and huge, black eyes that glittered darkly as it watched the two men.

"I am sick and in pain!" groaned the creature. "I will make you pay dearly for the suffering you have caused me." It scuttled around the pool of sunlight that Raiko and Tsuna had created by prying away the chamber roof stone by stone.

Then Raiko dropped to the floor below and battled the monster, keeping always in the square of light. The creature charged and retreated and charged again, but it was afraid of the sunlight that glinted off Raiko's armor and helmet and lay like a band of fire along his sword's blade.

Still the battle raged for more than an hour, before Raiko dispatched the monster with a blow of his sword that sent the creature's head rolling across the den. It came to rest beside a pile of human bones and skulls that showed how many unfortunate subjects of the Emperor had fallen victim to the monster.

Carrying the monster's head on a pole between them, Raiko and Tsuna returned to the Emperor's court, where they were highly praised and richly rewarded for their courage.

The Halloween Pony

(from a French folktale)

Grandmother put another log on the fire. Outside the little house which was not far from the sea, the wind was howling so fiercely that it set the windows rattling. "Listen to that!" said the old woman. "There's a storm brewing for sure."

She stirred the coals in the fireplace with a heavy poker until the new log caught and began to blaze. Satisfied, she turned to her three grandsons, who were sitting on the floor gazing thoughtfully into the flames. "Besides," she added, "this is Halloween. Witches are abroad tonight, and the goblins, who are their servants, are wandering about in all sorts of disguises, looking for children to snatch away."

But Tom, the eldest boy, said, "I won't stay here, frightened of a little wind and old stories. I promised Colette I'd call on her tonight. She swore she wouldn't get a wink of sleep, if I didn't visit her before the moon had gone down."

"I have to go and catch lobsters and crabs," said the middle boy, Louis. "Not all the witches and goblins in the world will keep me from that."

All three brothers announced they were going out for one reason or another and ignored the warnings of their

Grandmother. Only the youngest child hesitated a minute, when she said to him, "You stay with me, my little Richard, and I'll tell you stories of fairylands and magic animals."

But he wanted to pick blackberries by the moonlight, and so he ran out after his brothers.

He caught up with them on the rise, beneath the old oak tree.

"Grandmother talks about wind and storm, but I've never seen the weather finer or the sky more clear," said Louis, "I'll bring home plenty of crabs and lobsters to-night."

"See how big the moon is," said Tom. "Perhaps I can coax Colette to go for a walk with me."

Then Richard, who was starting for the blackberry patch, suddenly cried, "Look!" and he pointed to a little black pony standing quietly at the foot of the hill.

"Oh, ho!" said Louis, "that's old Frederic's pony; it must have escaped from its stable and is going down for a drink at the horse pond."

"Now, now, my pretty little pony," said Tom, going up and patting the creature with his hand, "you mustn't run away; I'll lead you to the pond myself."

With these words, he jumped on the pony's back.

"Take me, too," called Louis, and his brother helped him up.

"Don't leave me behind!" cried Richard, and his brothers helped him mount. Soon all three were astride the little black pony, which waited patiently till they had settled themselves. Tom clung to the pony's neck; Louis held Tom's waist; and Richard held Louis's shirt.

"Now, giddup!" urged Tom, and the little pony headed directly for the horse pond.

On their way, each brother met a friend and invited him to mount the pony. Soon there were six boys, holding to one another and laughing. The pony didn't seem to mind the extra weight but pranced merrily along under the brilliant moon.

The faster it trotted, the more the boys enjoyed the fun. They dug their heels into the pony's sides and called out, "Gallop, little horse! You've got six of the bravest riders in the world on your back!"

Soon they were racing along through the grassy fields near the seashore. The wind rose, sending clouds scudding across the face of the moon and whipping the pony's long black mane back across the eyes of the boys in front. Very close now, they could hear the waves pounding against the rocky shore.

The pony did not mind the noise at all. Instead of going to the horse pond, he circled around and cantered rapidly toward the seashore.

Louis, the middle brother, began to regret his wish to catch crabs and lobsters, and Richard, the youngest, found that he was no longer interested in blackberries. Both held onto their seats on the pony that was galloping at breakneck speed down toward the beach.

The eldest boy, Tom, seized the madly charging pony by the mane and tried to make it turn around. But he tugged and pulled in vain, for the pony galloped, fast as the howling wind, straight on toward the sea, pausing only when the first waves splashed over its hoofs.

The six riders thought to slip off the pony's back, while it lingered at the water's edge; but they found they were stuck fast to the creature's back.

Then, rearing up once, the little black pony neighed loudly, ran back and forth through the sea foam gleefully, then suddenly charged into the billowing waves, while its riders cried out in terror.

"The pony is bewitched!" wailed Tom. "We should have listened to Grandmother's warning."

The pony advanced farther and farther into the sea; the waves rose higher and higher until they covered the children's heads and the pony vanished beneath the swells.

Some say the children were drowned; some say the goblin pony carried them to a strange city of coral and pearl at the bottom of the sea. But they were never seen on dry land again.

Notes on Sources

THE ROBBER BRIDEGROOM. This is a favorite tale from the Brothers Grimm, which has frequently been translated. I've shortened it a bit, edited a few incidents, but have kept the general thrust of the story intact.

JACK FROST. I have freely adapted this traditional Russian tale, including incidents from several variant readings. This "red-nosed" Jack Frost is not the good-natured sprite who paints traceries of frost on winter windows: he is the blood-chilling, potentially deadly embodiment of a fierce Russian winter, when icy winds, blinding snow, and remorseless cold threaten death by freezing to the unfortunate.

THE WATERFALL OF GHOSTS. The story was originally published in English under the title "Yurei-Daki" in Lafcadio Hearn's *Kottō: Being Japanese Curios with Sundry Cobwebs*, first issued by the Macmillan Company, New York City, in 1902. Hearn (1850–1905) drew on old Japanese books for the ghostly tales in this volume. The writings of Lafcadio Hearn have been reissued in uniform paperback editions by Charles E. Tuttle Company, Rutland, Vermont, and Tokyo, Japan.

THE GHOST'S CAP. A retelling of an Icelandic folktale, "White Cap," originally gathered by Jón Árnason (1819–88), a librarian and teacher who assembled the monumental *Icelandic Legends* (1864), translated by George Powell and Eiríkur Magnússon, two volumes, second series, London: Longmans, Green and Co., 1866. Reprinted in *Scandinavian Folk and Fairy Tales* (1984) edited by Claire Booss, New York: Avenel Books, distributed by Crown, New York. I have enhanced this story with material from parallel tales from the Scandinavian and Russian.

THE WITCH CAT. This is a favorite American tale of witchcraft, yet another play upon the theme of shape shifting (see notes on the stories "The Loup-Garou" and "Brother and Sister"). Numerous variants of this story have found their way into folk literature; and I have drawn on several of the more interesting retellings for this version, including Nancy Roberts's excellent account in her *Ghosts of the Carolinas*.

THE GREEN MIST. Derived from Mrs. M. C. Balfour's account in her *Legends of the Lincolnshire Cars*, published in 1891, reprinted at length in Katherine

Briggs's *An Encyclopedia of Fairies,* Pantheon Books, a division of Random House, New York City, copyright 1976. (Originally published as *A Dictionary of Fairies* by Allen Lane, Penguin Books, London.)

THE CEGUA. I have created this original story around the horrific image of *La Cegua,* an apparition described in the tale of that name by Maximo Soto Hall (1871–1941), reprinted in *Leyendas de Costa Rica,* gathered by Victor H. Lizano, published by Soley & Valverde, San Jose, Costa Rica, in 1941. The name of this demon with an animal's head suggests the Spanish verb "cegar," "to blind" that also has the metaphorical meaning "to darken the light of reason" or "to make mad." It also suggests "yegua," or "mare." Such ghostly encounters (a man riding past a cemetery suddenly finds a skeleton seated behind him; a taxi driver picks up a spectre) form the basis of Hispanic folktales grouped under the heading "el pasajero del más allá"—"the passenger from the beyond."

THE GHOSTLY LITTLE GIRL. A much expanded version of an account found in Randall A. Reinstedt's *Ghostly Tales of Old Monterey.* The city of Monterey was California's historic first capital, and Mr. Reinstedt has explored its rich vein of ghostly lore in the work cited above and in his *Ghosts, Bandits, & Legends of Old Monterey.*

THE MIDNIGHT MASS OF THE DEAD. A considerably reworked and expanded version of a story collected by Peter Christen Asbjørnsen (1812–85), a lifelong student of Norse folklore, and first published in Norway in 1870 in Asbjørnsen's *Norske Huldreeventyr og Folksagn* (1845), accounts of dealings with spirit creatures from Norse folk traditions. Experts cite some twenty-five variants of this legend in Norway alone—and versions are familiar throughout north-central Europe.

TAILYPO. This is my own version of a classic American story, sometimes known as "Tailypoe," which has been retold countless numbers of times, with West Virginia or Tennessee as the preferred setting.

LADY ELEANORE'S MANTLE. This is a substantially edited version of the Nathaniel Hawthorne story of the same title, which was first published in *The Democratic Review,* December 1838. It was later included, in a much abbreviated form, in Charles M. Skinner's *Myths and Legends of Our Own Land,* two volumes, Philadelphia and London: J. B. Lippincott, first published in 1896. Reissued by Singing Tree Press, Book Tower, Detroit, in 1969.

THE SOLDIER AND THE VAMPIRE. A considerably reworked version of a traditional Russian folktale available in several translations. I have selected key incidents from various sources and have rearranged events and chronology to tighten the pacing and heighten the dramatic effect. For translations of the original tale, the reader might consult the version in *The World's Great Folktales,* arranged and edited by James R. Foster, New York: Harper & Brothers, 1953, or the version in *Passport to the Supernatural,* Bernhardt J. Hurwood, New York: Taplinger, 1972.

THE SKELETON'S DANCE. Originally published in Keigo Seki's *Nihon no Mukashi-banashi (Japanese Folktales)*, three volumes, Tokyo: Iwanami Shoten, 1956–57. The editor of the University of Chicago's selection of translations from the complete work comments that twelve versions of the tale have been recorded in Japan.

SCARED TO DEATH. I have adapted Margaret Rhett Martin's version of this story, which she has titled "The Leaning Tombstone," from her collection, *Charleston Ghosts*, University of South Carolina Press, copyright 1963.

SWALLOWED ALIVE. This bit of Derbyshire folklore is adapted from the account John Bunyan (1628–1688) includes in his *The Life and Death of Mr. Badman Presented to the World in a Familiar Dialogue Between Mr. Wiseman and Mr. Attentive* (1680). In this work by the author of *Pilgrim's Progress*, Mr. Wiseman presents the story of Dorothy Mately as an actual historic occurrence for the instruction of Mr. Attentive and a warning against "such wickedness [as] cursing and swearing."

THE DEACON'S GHOST. Retold from a tale, "The Deacon of Myrká," in *Icelandic Legends* by Jón Arnason (see note on "The Ghost's Cap"). According to Icelandic folklore, white wizards lived in the north, where they continued to practice pagan magic, away from Christian settlements—presumably such a wizard finally laid the ghost to rest.

NUCKELAVEE. Adapted from *Orkney Folklore and Traditions*, a collection of articles by Walter Traill Dennison (died in 1894), who originally published them in the *Scottish Antiquary* in the 1890s. These pieces were subsequently gathered and edited by Ernest W. Marwick and are available in a reprint edition from Herald Press, Kirkwall, Orkney, 1961.

The name "Nuckelavee" translates as "Devil from the Sea," (coming from the same root as "Old Nick," the Devil). Dennison obtained his story firsthand from "Thomas," who claimed to have survived this close encounter of the nightmare kind.

THE ADVENTURE OF THE GERMAN STUDENT. Edited and adapted from Washington Irving's *Tales of a Traveller*, first published in 1824. This selection is one of the supernatural stories appearing in the first section of the book, "Strange Stories by a Nervous Gentleman," and is considered by some critics to be Irving's most terrifying tale. The story, he wrote, was "founded on an anecdote related to me as existing somewhere in French," but he admitted he was never able to discover its source.

BILLY MOSBY'S NIGHT RIDE. I have elaborated considerably upon the account entitled "Francis Woolcott" in Charles M. Skinner's *Myths and Tales of Our Own Land* (op. cit.).

THE HUNTER IN THE HAUNTED FOREST. A combining and reworking of three brief Teton Sioux tales originally included in *Myths and Legends of the Great Plains*, selected and edited by Katharine Berry Judson, A. C. McClurg & Co., Chicago, 1913.

BROTHER AND SISTER. In retelling this favorite African traditional tale, I have borrowed from variants of a story popular in Kenya, Zambia, and Malawi, fleshing out my version with details from collateral readings. I have changed the familiar ending, where the brother causes a drum or wooden bowl or a miniature boat to float into the air while he and his sister hold on to it and escape the werebeast, in favor of a pursuit and escape that relies on human abilities rather than inexplicably acquired magical powers.

THE LOVERS OF DISMAL SWAMP. My own version of a classic American folktale dating back to colonial times, set in and around the Dismal Swamp, near Portsmouth, Virginia. I have combined several accounts of the tale, including elements from the Irish poet Thomas Moore's poem "The Lake of the Dismal Swamp," composed during a visit to the United States in 1803, and Charles M. Skinner's similarly titled prose version in his *Myths and Legends of Our Own Land* (op. cit.).

BONELESS. An original story suggested by several brief, historic accounts cited in Katherine Briggs's indispensable *An Encyclopedia of Fairies,* (op. cit.).

THE DEATH WALTZ. Retold from *Myths and Tales of Our Own Land* by Charles M. Skinner (op. cit.).

THE GHOST OF MISERY HILL. Expanded from the tale "The Spook of Misery Hill," included in *Myths and Legends of Our Own Land,* by Charles M. Skinner (op. cit.).

THE LOUP-GAROU. A French-Canadian legend adapted from an 1894 account in dialect originally published in *Danvis Folks,* by Rowland E. Robinson, Houghton Mifflin Company, Boston and New York. It has been reprinted in B. A. Botkin's *A Treasury of New England Folklore,* Crown Publishers, copyright 1947, 1965.

The term *loup-garou* comes from the Old French *leu garoul: leu =* wolf + *garoul =* werewolf.

THE GOLEM. This is my own "Golem" story, based on a reading of several of the medieval Jewish tales of the clay figure brought to life, which has formed a popular theme in legend and literature.

The two most popular accounts are the *Golem of Chelm,* which tells how Rabbi Elijah of that town created such a creature, but was so appalled by its destructive tendencies that he removed the magic parchment he had placed in the creature's forehead and it crumbled into dust. The second account, the *Golem of Prague,* tells how Rabbi Yehuda Loew brought the clay being into existence, to protect the Jews of that city from persecution. When its work was done, the rabbi returned it to a lifeless clay statue again; according to legend, it remains hidden in a synagogue in Prague, waiting to be summoned to life when it is needed again.

The Hebrew word *golem* refers to anything incomplete or not fully formed, since the creature was never completely human. Some critics have suggested that legends of the *golem* contributed to the background of ideas Mary Shelley drew upon when writing her 1818 novel *Frankenstein*, but no clear-cut evidence has surfaced to indicate she was familiar with this body of folklore.

LAVENDER. This popular American ghost story pops up in versions all across the United States, from New Jersey to California. A prime example of "urban folklore," the events are frequently presented as having happened to someone the storyteller has known personally.

THE GOBLIN SPIDER. A Japanese traditional story, one of many built around the legendary hero Raiko, whose exploits are widely anthologized. This particular variant of the well-known "Goblin Spider Episode," is loosely based on a summary in *Myths and Legends of Japan* by F. Hadland Davis. Mr. Davis prefaced his account with the comment, "This version appears in the *Catalogue of Japanese and Chinese Paintings in the British Museum* by Dr. William Anderson." I have no date for the latter work.

THE HALLOWEEN PONY. Freely adapted from "The Goblin Pony," a French folktale retold by Andrew Lang in his *The Grey Fairy Book*, originally published by Longmans, Green and Company, London, 1900, and reprinted by Dover Publications, New York, in 1967.

ABOUT THE AUTHOR

Robert D. San Souci is the author of four previous children's books for Doubleday. After receiving his bachelor's degree in English from St. Mary's College in Moraga, California, and then completing two years of graduate study in education, Mr. San Souci pursued a career in publishing. He now writes full time from his home in the San Francisco Bay area of California.

ABOUT THE ARTIST

Katherine Coville has worked as a full-time illustrator for the past ten years. Her work in both full color and black and white has appeared in over twenty children's books. In her spare time the artist enjoys making miniature toys and dollhouses. The mother of three, Ms. Coville resides in Syracuse, New York.